BETWEEN WORLDS 2

THE DISTANCE

LORI WOLF-HEFFNER

HEAD IN THE GROUND PUBLISHING

Editing by Susan Fish, Heather Wright

Cover design by Fresh Design

All photographs from Shutterstock

Head in the Ground Publishing

Waterloo, Ontario, Canada

www.headintheground.com

 Created with Vellum

This book is dedicated to my mentor, Carol McCuaig, whose encouragement to write about my history helped create this series. Carol passed away February 22, 2018.

CHAPTER ONE

"Remember that time we put on fake tattoos and took fashion photos?" Juliana asked.

Rachel's face, spread out on the screen of Juliana's laptop, lit up in a smile. It was a thing best friends would always remember. Even if they lived in different cities now. "Our parents were not happy about that!"

Juliana smiled, too, but then her cheeks turned red. "I'm just glad the tattoos washed off. I honestly didn't realize that one was a cross. I thought it was a 't' and I wanted something for 'tap.' I don't know why they don't make tap tattoos."

"You and me both," Rachel agreed.

Juliana had forgotten about the whole mess until she began reorganizing her photos just before Rachel called from Calgary. She remembered the awkwardness of the lecture from both of their parents. The girls had thought tattoos would be cool and had wet them and put them on their wrists. The pictures they'd taken weren't for any particular purpose; they had just wanted to have some fun. But their parents had panicked, thinking the tattoos were permanent.

"I miss having you around," Rachel said.

"I miss you, too," Juliana replied.

It had only been a week since Juliana and her parents had driven halfway across the country to move in with and look after Juliana's grandfather, who was in the early stages of dementia. Only a week since she had had friends to laugh or be embarrassed with: all her dance and school friends were back in Calgary. Although she had no family there—Dad didn't have any at all, and Mom's was here in Kitchener—Calgary was still her home.

"Show me your room," Rachel said.

Juliana rolled her eyes at the idea of carrying her laptop around her tiny bedroom.

"No, really," Rachel insisted. "I can't be there in person, so give me the tour."

Juliana unplugged her laptop and lifted it up. "This is my bed," Juliana said, pointing the camera toward her single bed, tucked against the wall, with her duvet smoothed out and pillow set properly on top.

"Beautifully made, of course," Rachel said. "Here's mine."

Juliana saw a pile of blankets at the foot of Rachel's bed threatening to teeter over at any moment. "I wouldn't expect any less!" she said. "And these are my bookshelves—"

"Let me guess: organized alphabetically by author?"

"Aha!" Juliana said, playfully pointing a finger at her best friend as though she'd caught her in a trap. "Nope! By title. I thought I'd try something different."

"Well, Ms. Roth, I'm very impressed," Rachel replied. "You may be thousands of kilometres away, but you're still as organized as ever. I mean, the moving truck just came yesterday! Oh wait! Stop right there!"

Juliana's laptop faced an empty wall. "What?"

"That wallpaper is to die for!"

The girls broke out in a simultaneous giggle. Juliana knew exactly what Rachel meant: the wallpaper had an awful floral design on a cream background, and the pattern was separated by wide stripes of deep green velvet. Or so it felt, anyway: it was fuzzy.

Juliana set the laptop back down on her desk. "Oh!" she said. "There's one thing I haven't shown you yet." She stepped away from her desk, opened up her nightstand drawer, and carefully pulled out her great-grandmother's book of drawings. "I've told you about it, but you haven't seen it." Juliana opened the book to the first page—its old spine complaining at being disturbed—and held up the drawing of her great-grandmother's kitchen.

"Wow...that's not your work is it?"

Juliana feigned indignation. "How long have we known each other?" She lowered the book so Rachel could see her again and then smiled. "No. This is that book of drawings I told you about. This is the kitchen my great-grandmother grew up in. The floor was made of dirt and chaff—that's the stalk from wheat—and they had no phone. It really looks like they lived in a Third World country, but it was Europe."

"Europe? I thought Europe was rich? Isn't it super expensive to go there? That's why all the famous people live there."

Juliana shrugged.

"What else is in there?" Rachel asked.

"Tons. Take a look."

Juliana held up the book and slowly turned the next pages: a pair of mittens, a party of some sort, and a drawing of an envelope. Then she lowered the book again.

"There are tons of these drawings in here."

"And you found it in a box in the basement?"

"Mmm. And this really old set of encyclopedias. All on Christmas Eve. An otherwise totally embarrassing night for me."

Juliana heard the hallway floor outside her room creak as slow steps made their way along. Opa didn't knock like her parents did, but the rhythm of his walk had the same effect. He entered her room.

"Hi, Opa," Juliana said. "I'm talking to my best friend, Rachel."

Opa paused for a moment, as though he was trying to think, and then his eyes opened wide. "In Calgary?"

"Yeah!" She leaned out of the way so Opa could see the screen.

"*Na, so was!*" he said in German. Juliana didn't understand the words, but his body language showed his amazement.

"Rachel, this is my grandfather."

"Hello!" Rachel smiled and waved.

Opa smiled in return. He brushed his hand over his bald head. "I'm not as attractive as I once was," he said with a sheepish grin.

They laughed.

"I'm showing Rachel your mom's book of drawings."

The book was still open to the drawing of a party: a woman in a simple but formal dress was surrounded by other women in similar dresses, all reaching out to hold a bonnet.

"I haven't seen a wedding ceremony like that in many, many years!" Opa said.

"That's a wedding?" Juliana asked.

Opa nodded. "The bride is getting her *haube*."

"Her what?"

Opa opened his mouth wide and enunciated the word. "*Hau-be*."

Juliana followed his lips' movements. "How-ba?"

Opa nodded.

Although now satisfied that she could say it, Juliana had no idea what the word meant.

Opa pointed to the bonnet. "That's a *haube*. It's what every girl wanted when she grew up. Once the wedding ceremony was over, others at the wedding sang a song and put it on her head. It meant she was married and now a woman. She'd then wear it in the home or under her headscarf outside the home."

On the other side of the screen, Rachel's eyes got wide. "She wasn't a woman until she was married?"

Opa nodded. "That's how it was back then."

"What did boys do to show they were finally men?" Rachel asked.

Opa paused and then shrugged. "I don't know. I've never thought about it."

Juliana studied the drawing more closely. Her great-grandmother had drawn the scene in a way that she could show the back of the bonnet: it was white and looked like it fit close to the head. Juliana fingered her brown hair, having a hard time imagining tying it up under a bonnet. She loved styling it, sometimes braiding it, other times curling it. She especially loved the elegance straightening her hair gave her.

Opa turned the page back to the image of the mittens:

the mittens were worn by one pair of hands with another pair of hands pulling at them.

"Ah, that reminds me," he said. "We had fresh snow this morning. I should check the basement. Maybe I need to switch the blankets."

At Rachel's confused look, Juliana explained. "There's a crack in the foundation, and with the warmer winters here, water sometimes leaks in. So he's got blankets on the floor there just in case."

"I called Annie and told her not to come shovel today," he said.

"That's my aunt," Juliana explained. "They live literally around the corner and she always comes here with one or two of my cousins to shovel Opa's driveway and sidewalk."

"That's so cool," Rachel said. "My family lives all over Calgary, so it's hard to get together that much."

"I'm very lucky like that," Opa said. He patted Juliana on the head. "And now that Yulika has moved here, my life couldn't be better." Without saying another word, he turned around and left the room.

"'Yulika'? Oh my god, Juliana! Your grandfather's so cute! Especially with his accent! My family's been here for so long, we don't have anything cool like an accent."

Juliana nodded. "I know. He's the only grandparent I have, and I'm just getting to know him now. It's sad but also good."

"But your aunt couldn't look after your grandfather? I mean, if they live just around the corner..."

"She's also got six kids, and even though two are already in their twenties, she's still too busy. I think with us moving in, Mom and her sister and brother don't have to worry as much about Opa, because now there's always someone to help him."

Rachel's face became dead serious. "I guess that makes sense. I still have all my grandparents. If I had only one, I'd probably take extra care of them, too."

"Dad never talks about his family, and I'm only starting to get to know Mom's. It's a lot different when you meet them in person."

"You start dance soon, right?" Rachel asked, switching to a different topic.

Juliana's face lit up. "Tomorrow, actually! I can hardly wait."

"Just remember who your best friend is."

Juliana's heart almost broke. "Rachel, how could you think that? You'll always be my best friend, even when we're half a country apart!"

She looked at the screen. Even though they had talked this way forever, it was different when it was the only way they could see each other. In order to look each other in the eyes, they had to look at their screens, which meant they weren't looking each other in the eyes. It felt odd and made

Rachel feel farther away or like Juliana was watching Rachel talk to someone else.

"Listen, Rachel, I should probably get going. Opa might need some help, especially if those blankets are wet."

"Best friends forever?"

"Absolutely. Best friends forever."

"I know your dance practice tomorrow will be stellar."

"You think so?"

"I've got a really good feeling about it."

CHAPTER TWO

*E*lisabeth wiped her hands on her apron. It was Sunday, January 11, 1920, in Semlak, Romania, the second Sunday of the new decade. Sadly the new decade was not beginning in peace: Romania was still at war with Hungary. However, as Elisabeth knew, it would be the year that would complete Semlak's transition from being part of Hungary to Romania, as had been officially announced by Romania's king just after Christmas.

Elisabeth didn't have time to think about the bigger world: in the weeks after her father's move to America, she was now in charge of the household.

"That girl never picks up after herself!" she mumbled under her breath. Anna, the second oldest child in the family at nine, had left her new red mittens on the ground again. Knowing her sister was already finding it difficult to continue in their day-to-day lives while Tata was away in America to earn money, Elisabeth picked them up and ran to put them in the back room where the girls' winter shawls lay folded up. She hoped to save Anna from punishment.

Maybe Anna can make a promise to be tidier this year, she thought.

"What is so urgent that you have to run?" Mammi asked from the front room, where she was braiding the younger girls' hair for church.

"Just tidying up!" Elisabeth replied.

"Did Anna leave her mittens on the floor again?"

Elisabeth shot a quick glance up at the crucifix that hung over the doorway between the back room and the kitchen. *Please forgive me*, she prayed. "No," she lied.

She heard a slap and Anna began to whimper. Within moments, Mammi came stomping through the house, from the front room, through the kitchen, and into the back room, her waist-long brown hair swishing as she marched, and her black overskirt and layers of underskirts having a hard time keeping up with her speed. "One more lie like that and you'll be kneeling in the box of corn!" Mammi threatened her oldest child.

Trembling with regret, Elisabeth nodded. "I'm sorry." She knew Mammi was also finding life without her husband hard, and Elisabeth had promised herself at

Christmas that she would do her best to help her family instead of causing them trouble.

Elisabeth gave up the hope that Anna would try to be neater. Instead, she made a mental note to remind Anna to pick up her mittens from now on. If Anna didn't remember after that slap.

Mammi looked Elisabeth up and down, let out a short grunt, and returned to the other girls and Luki, their only brother.

The family hadn't heard from Tata yet, and it had been six weeks. They had expected him to be underway for about two weeks, give or take a few days, but to write immediately once he'd arrived. How much longer would they have to wait? No one in the Schuhmacher household said anything, but Elisabeth could feel it: they were all worried something had happened to him.

Anna had stopped whimpering, but now she let out little shrieks as Mammi jabbed hairpins into her braids to pin them on her head.

"Now, out, all of you," Mammi ordered. "I have to get myself ready. Lissika, make sure they're ready for church."

Anna, Luki, and their youngest sister, Rosina, scrambled out of the front room and into the kitchen, and Elisabeth knew she had very little time to get her younger siblings dressed and looking impeccable before Mammi finished whipping her own hair into a flat bun on top of her head and covering it with her *haube* and headscarf.

The children rushed into the back room to put on their boots—which Anna had polished—and their clothing for outdoors. Luki pulled on a coat, hat, and new black mittens, while his sisters wrapped themselves in elaborately crafted shawls, simple, white headscarves, and mittens. Anna stared for a moment at the red mittens she had left on the floor earlier and then looked down at the dirt-and-chaff floor.

"Sorry," she mumbled, barely loud enough for Elisabeth to hear.

Every German farmer's household in Semlak had the same floor, and Elisabeth knew other families had messy children, too. Anna certainly wasn't the only one to leave her things lying around. Elisabeth dusted off any bits of dirt from the mittens.

"I'm sorry, too," Elisabeth whispered back. "I'll try to remind you next time."

Anna nodded.

The children put on their leather boots, and Elisabeth helped Rosina, who was only six, to tie hers up.

"Are you all ready?" Mammi asked as she swung open the door and emerged from the front room.

Dressed all in black, from the top of her head to her feet, Mammi looked almost regal. Her black *tschurak*—a thin, fitted jacket that covered her hips—hugged her bodice, and her skirts gave her an air of authority that no unmarried girl could have. And just sticking out from under her headscarf were the edges of her *haube*. Elisabeth could hardly wait herself to marry in a year or two—if all went well—and to be able to dress as all the married German women in Semlak and other villages in their region, called the Banat, did.

ELISABETH, ANNA, ROSINA, AND MAMMI SAT ON THE RIGHT side of the church, and Luki sat with Tata's brother Konrad-Bátschi on the left. Next to Konrad-Bátschi sat his two sons, Georg and Samuel, who were much older than Luki. Georg had fought in the war but had not come home until a month after the big conflicts had ended, in December 1918. Samuel had contracted polio as a child, and his limp left him unfit for war.

Elisabeth looked around the women's side of the church and politely nodded to almost everyone she knew, including her aunt, Konrad-Bátschi's wife, Margarethe-Néni.

Pastor Fröhlich read intently from Martin Luther's Bible. As he read, Elisabeth tried her best to listen to Luther's words, but all she could think about was how much she longed to read at home again, from both her father's encyclopedia and the family's humble but important collection of Luther's works. But with all her new chores and responsibilities since Mammi had taken over making and repairing shoes in Tata's absence, Elisabeth had no time during the day or evening to read. And now she would be busy helping with wedding preparations: Konrad-Bátschi's youngest daughter, Susanna, would marry Schubkegel Adam in a few weeks. That meant Elisabeth would join a group of girls and young women from Susi's family and friends to cook for several hundred guests and sew whatever the bride and bridal party needed.

Jesus only had to teach, she thought.

Anna poked her in the side, pulling Elisabeth back to the present: everyone was already standing for the next hymn, so Elisabeth jumped up and joined in.

"Welcome, Lissika! Welcome, Anna! It's so good to see you!" Their cousin Gretche, older than Elisabeth by a few years and already married, kissed each girl on the cheek and stepped back into the kitchen so both Schuhmacher siblings could come inside and take off their boots at the door. Six other women and older girls, all of whom Elisabeth and Anna knew, stood around the table and either nodded or waved.

Susanna, the bride-to-be and the youngest of this part of the Schuhmacher family, rushed to the doorway and also kissed each girl on both cheeks. At sixteen, turning seventeen later that year, she was someone Elisabeth looked up to now.

Konrad-Bátschi and Georg were out back in their blacksmith shop. As was customary, Margarethe-Néni was in charge of preparing the food and managing the group of ten or so women and girls at her house today.

"It's wonderful to be here." Elisabeth smiled as she leaned a bag of flour, a wooden rolling pin, and a pastry board against the wall so that she could remove her boots. She appreciated the chance to spend time outside her own home for a few hours, though she dreaded the actual tasks they'd have to do. And the gossip.

Anna laid a basket of eggs and her rolling pin and pastry board against the wall, too, and then set her mittens next to them so she could untie her boots.

Both girls slipped into their house shoes and passed their shawls to Gretche. Elisabeth then gently nudged Anna to remind her about her mittens.

"May I leave my mittens here?" Anna asked, pointing to a table near the lime-painted brick stove. "Some boys threw snowballs at me on the way here."

Gretche's smile stretched from cheek to cheek. "Oh, those boys can be bad, can't they? Of course, you may. But don't put them too close: you don't want the wool to shrink."

Anna nodded and placed her mittens on the table. Elisabeth also gave her approval and both girls picked up their tools and ingredients and carried them over to the kitchen table.

The door opened behind them, letting in a blast of cold air. "Ah, Lissika! Anna!" Their aunt came in, carrying a basket of eggs she had retrieved from the cellar out back. The sisters greeted their aunt and kissed her on both cheeks. "It's so nice to have two people from your family join us!"

Margarethe-Néni's comment was not a compliment, and Elisabeth knew it. When Tata had first announced that he was leaving, back in October, his brother and sister-in-law had repeatedly complained that he was needed here. As much as Elisabeth had agreed with them and had even prayed that Tata would listen to them, she now understood that he loved his family with all his heart and that it was his love that took him away. Margarethe-Néni's "compliment" was actually an attempt to quietly insult Elisabeth's family.

"Mammi sends her regrets, but she has to keep an eye on little Rosina and Luki," Elisabeth said in the politest tone she could manage. She didn't add that her mother needed to rest after all the hours spent making shoes this past week in the cold, dark workshop. But at almost thirty-five years old, Mammi was already halfway through her life, God willing, and had enough on her plate as it was. "But she has promised to bake her famous coffee cake in time for the wedding, and she's also happy to look after any *minor* shoe repairs for the wedding party."

The emphasis on the word minor was Elisabeth's: she knew her aunt would take advantage of Mammi's offer if Elisabeth didn't clearly explain the details.

"That's very kind of her," Margarethe-Néni replied. She handed the eggs to her daughter, who set them on the floor by the table, which was covered with a white, handwoven, linen tablecloth and crowded with pastry boards. "Susi's wedding will have hundreds of guests," she said, "so good shoes will be necessary. No need to give Meier Josef something to gossip about."

Elisabeth nodded in agreement: her aunt was right about that.

Margarethe-Néni clapped her hands. "To work!"

Elisabeth smiled to keep pushing her real feelings down: of all the cooking chores she had to do, she disdained making special noodles the most. Rolling out the dough so flat you could almost read the Bible through it often left Elisabeth with a sore back.

And now she would be doing that for hours.

"Elisabeth!" Eva emerged from the back room, adjusting her black headscarf. "I'm so sorry I didn't greet you right when you arrived! I just had to fold up some tea towels and put them away."

Eva was Georg's second wife, only eighteen years old, young compared to Georg's twenty-nine years. With a wife so young, she could provide him with many children, and because Georg would inherit Konrad-Bátschi's blacksmith shop one day, he could provide stability for their family. Eva wouldn't even have to work the fields except at harvest time, when all children were taken out of school and every available hand was required to bring in the crops for the winter.

"Thank you for coming to help, even though you're not part of the wedding. That's so kind of you!"

Elisabeth again forced a smile, though part of her wanted to roll dough over Eva's mouth. Living with her in-laws had already turned her into one of them, it seemed.

"I'm happy to help out anyway I can, of course," Elisabeth replied, silently asking Jesus to forgive her for lying. And for her bad thoughts.

"Anna!" Eva continued. "It's wonderful to see you! I can't believe how much you've grown!"

Elisabeth tried hard not to roll her eyes. They saw one another at church every week and here was Eva, talking as though they hadn't seen each other in months, something that would rarely happen in Semlak. If anyone left for long periods of time, it was usually for war, America, or Heaven.

Eva helped the other girls and women move their pastry boards over to make room for the two sisters. Elisabeth greeted the others at the table, rolled up her sleeves, and dug her hands into an open bag of flour.

"What do you think about Wagner Anni?" one of the older girls asked.

"Didn't she look just terrible?" another replied. "Her

nose is now so crooked after her accident." Everyone giggled, leaving Elisabeth feeling terrible about the poor girl.

"Jesus says we are to be nice to one another," she said.

The other girls looked at each other uneasily, so Elisabeth tried to change the subject. "What did you think about Pastor Fröhlich's sermon yesterday? I'm certain he was talking about trying to remain with Hungary. Did you hear that, too?"

The only answer she got was more blank stares. Although their reaction was expected, Elisabeth had hoped someone might say something in reply. She couldn't bear an afternoon of mean chatter. But after an awkward silence, Gretche returned to the topic of Wagner Anni, this time disdaining her shoes, and the gossip about the poor girl continued. Elisabeth sighed and wished the men were there so she could listen in on their conversations instead.

CHAPTER THREE

*J*uliana rubbed her eyes, stretched her hands and feet as far away from her core as she could, then grabbed her left leg, straightened it, pulled it as close to her face as she could before letting it go and repeating the stretch with her right leg. Then she rolled over onto her stomach and folded her legs back so that her heels touched her bum. She grabbed her ankles and pulled everything toward the ceiling, bending her body backwards into a doughnut. Finally awake from her morning stretch, she let herself flop back onto her bed. Her ears now awake, too, she heard the wind howling outside.

Snow piled up in the corners of her small bedroom window. She sat up, rubbed her eyes again, and shivered. She grabbed a sweater off the back of her desk chair and stumbled out to the kitchen.

"*Guten morgen*, Yulika," Opa said, using his nickname for her. He peeled himself a banana, starting from the bottom. He was always up and wide awake before she was even conscious of anything.

"Good morning," she replied. She had assumed that was what those words meant, and since he never looked confused when she replied in English, she had decided to go with it.

"We got thirty centimetres of snow overnight," he said. "Roads are closed, and the city wants no one on the streets so they can plough."

"What?"

Juliana walked past the kitchen table to the front door, which opened into the kitchen, yanked on it to open it, and stared outside.

Their small street, which had houses on this side and apartment buildings on the other, was covered in a thick blanket of snow.

"It looks like packing snow!" Juliana exclaimed.

"You can make a snowman in the backyard," Opa said. "You're not going anywhere today, and no one will bother your snowman back there."

"Not going anywhere?"

Opa bit into his banana and pointed to the bowl of fruit, suggesting Juliana help herself. She grabbed an apple and washed it in the sink.

"Don't you have dance class today?" he asked.

Juliana was surprised by how much he remembered sometimes. She still wasn't entirely sure if he had dementia: sometimes she was certain he did, but what if his forgetfulness was just because he was getting old? He was already seventy. Even her teachers at school forgot things sometimes, and they were much younger.

"I do." She bit into the apple.

"They'll close it."

"Close it? But it's just snow!"

Juliana set the apple on the table, ran back to her bedroom, clicked her phone on, and called up her email. There was a message from Kitchener Dance Academy, her new studio.

Dear Juliana,

We regret to inform you that classes are cancelled today due to snow.

Regards,

Mrs. D. Laing

Juliana shook her head. Whoever this Mrs. D. Laing was, she didn't sound very friendly. Juliana had exchanged emails with her over the past couple of months, and each email sounded corporate. Hopefully it was just this Mrs. D. Laing who talked like that and not everyone at the studio. She tossed her phone back onto her bed and returned to the kitchen.

"You were right, Opa. I got a message on my phone."
She slumped into a chair at the table and bit into her apple.
"It's like Kitchener's never dealt with snow before!"

"How does your phone tell you that?" Opa asked as he
handed her a plate.

Juliana smiled. "It's not that my phone told me, it's that
I got an email."

Opa nodded, but Juliana could tell he didn't understand. "It's like a letter, but instead of getting it from the
mailbox, I get it from my phone. Just like you can call
someone and leave a message, you can also type something
to someone and send it to them."

Opa's eyes lit up and Juliana saw that he understood.
She was beginning to learn how to explain things to him:
how she bought her music online, or, like yesterday, how
she stayed in touch with Rachel. Maybe she could set up an
email account for Opa someday.

Juliana finished her apple and got what she needed for
a bowl of cereal. "Do you want some, too?"

"Cornflakes, please," he said.

As Juliana retrieved bowls and spoons, Opa continued
to talk. "When they served us cornflakes on the boat, we
knew we were coming to the new world."

Juliana almost burst out laughing, but not in a mean
way. Cornflakes? The new world?

"It's all right," Opa said. "Laugh all you want. But it's

true. It meant we didn't have to grow our own food anymore."

Juliana chuckled. "But growing your own food is trendy."

Opa smiled and nodded. "I'll never understand that. Why would you want to spend all that time tending to plants when you could sit down, put your feet up, and watch television?"

Juliana had to agree: gardening wasn't her thing either.

BY MID-MORNING, JULIANA WAS ON THE TAP BOARD HER parents had given her as a Christmas gift, hammering to her own rhythm with her feet. Her parents, finally awake, were eating a leisurely breakfast and chatting away with Opa upstairs.

Juliana let the sounds of her tap shoes roll off her feet and onto the wooden board. If she heard anything uneven, like a cramp roll that went *da-de-de* instead of *da-da-de-de*, she slowed the step to improve her articulation.

A knock at the side door of the house—which was just up the stairs from where Juliana was in the basement—distracted her. She ran up to answer it.

It was Aunt Anne and Sophie, one of her aunt's numerous children and the one closest in age to Juliana, though two years younger. Sophie was also going blind, a fact that made Juliana nervous. The door opened onto a small landing with the basement below and the kitchen two steps up and to the left. How would Sophie come inside without falling down the stairs?

"We came over to shovel," Aunt Anne said.

Juliana nodded. "We could've looked after it." She stole a glance at Sophie and wondered how she'd shovel. How would she know where to put the snow?

"Katy told me that, but we do this all the time. And since your parents are returning to work in a few days, it made no sense to break the tradition."

"Come on in," Juliana said, trying hard to be friendly. She took a step back onto the top stair to give them room to enter and so she could catch Sophie should she come too close to the edge of the stairs. But they stayed outside.

"Hi, Annie!" Opa called from the kitchen.

Aunt Anne peeked in the door and up to the kitchen. "Hi, Tata! Katy, Paul!"

"You're early," Mom said. "Give us a sec and we'll help."

Aunt Anne waved her hand. "You guys just sit and enjoy while you can. We'll get this done in no time. If someone can just hand us the keys to the garage..."

"Yulika, top drawer, in the table, under the window," Opa said.

Juliana opened the drawer and found several keys on a ring, all gold with a square top. She held them up to Aunt Anne.

"Oh, I can never tell which one is the right one. Give them to Sophie—she'll figure it out."

Puzzled but not wanting to show it, Juliana handed the key ring to her cousin. Sophie fingered through one key after another and within a few seconds said, "Found it!" She held the apparently correct key in her hand, turned around, and walked back outside toward the detached garage.

"Won't she trip?" Juliana said before she could stop her thoughts from coming out of her mouth.

Aunt Anne's smile drooped and Juliana could feel her own cheeks burn. Too embarrassed to look at her family sitting in the kitchen, but wanting to do something to apologize, Juliana ran up through the kitchen and into the back hallway, where she tore off her dance shoes, jumped into her boots, whipped on her winter jacket, red gloves, beige scarf, and multicoloured tuque, and headed outside.

"I'll help," she said as she stepped into the garage.

"Just watch you don't put out your back," Aunt Anne warned. "This snow is heavy."

Juliana nodded.

"Excuse me." Sophie's voice told Juliana that she'd heard Juliana's question from a few minutes before. "Trippy blind person coming through."

No dance class, and now this. The day that was supposed to be the highlight of her holidays—especially after her failed Christmas Eve—began to feel like an exam where she was being tested on things she didn't know. She'd never talked to a blind person before. Juliana wanted to be nice, but based on Aunt Anne's and Sophie's reactions, her intentions weren't coming across as she intended.

Sophie slowly walked to the end of the driveway and began shovelling as though she could see. Juliana was confused.

"You don't have to stare at her," Aunt Anne whispered, startling Juliana.

"I'm...I'm really sorry," Juliana stammered. "And about before, too. I've never been around someone who's blind."

Aunt Anne's face relaxed. "I forget that sometimes it's new for people. Sophie has what's called juvenile macular degeneration, so she's not as blind as you're probably thinking: she's losing her sight in the middle of her field of vision."

Juliana nodded, though she didn't quite understand.

"Go online later and look it up. You'll find images that'll show you what she sees. But it means she has peripheral vision, so she can see things beside, above, and below her, but nothing in front of her. She can tell, for example, when she's following a wall, but she can't read a normal book."

Now Juliana understood why her cousin was so confident when she walked.

"But it also means she'll continue losing her sight for some time," Aunt Anne continued. "It progressed really fast when she was younger, and the ophthalmologist said it would keep going."

"You're talking about me, aren't you?" Sophie asked.

"Can she hear really far?" Juliana asked.

Aunt Anne chuckled. "No. She just pays more attention to sound: the fact that our voices are lowered and no one's talking to her tells her that we're talking about her." She called out to her daughter, "Just catching your cousin up on things."

Juliana knew she had to change the conversation: it was still morning and her day was already headed for a cliff. She moved over to one side of the single driveway and tried to push the shovel all the way across. By the time she got to the other side, though, she could barely lift it.

"You're right," she said. "This stuff is heavy."

"You don't get this in Calgary?" Sophie called over.

"We do, but my parents always had a service to shovel the driveway and sidewalk, and since Dad has no family, there was no one to shovel for either." Juliana paused for a moment as she thought back. "To be honest, I think the last time I shovelled snow was maybe...in grade four or five."

"Must have been nice!" Sophie said.

"It definitely was!"

Juliana looked over at her aunt and saw a smile on her face.

Can u talk?

No at restaurant but I can text u ok?

Juliana was relieved she could talk to Rachel. Aunt Anne and Sophie had left a couple of hours ago, and Juliana was still mortified about what she'd said. She adjusted the ice pack on her lower back and then kept texting.

Feel like an idiot

U r NOT an idiot! What happened?

Said something stupid to Sophie

???

Too much to text just stupid day so far

There was a pause, and Juliana began to wonder if Rachel also thought she was stupid. Then her phone rang. It was Rachel.

"I thought you couldn't talk."

"I told Dad you needed me, and we're still waiting for the food—we're having lunch at one of those fancy places —so he let me step out by the foyer, where this place has a nice fire burning."

"That's what my cheeks felt like outside today, in the midst of thirty centimetres of snow."

"Juliana, you have to tell me what happened."

Juliana recounted the entire story to Rachel, including how she was worried Sophie would fall down the stairs.

"And to finish it all off, my back is killing me from all that shovelling." She flipped the ice pack around.

"You're not supposed to use your back," Rachel said.

"Figured that out now, thank you, Einstein. But it's just been a crappy day and I could really use a best friend."

"Listen, Jules, your first dance practice got cancelled and you're still getting used to your mom's family. You've never had to deal with family before. Everything about this situation is totally new for you." She paused for a moment, and Juliana wondered if she was supposed to say something. She looked out the window in her bedroom and sighed. It hadn't even been a week yet, and she was homesick. How long would this last?

"Listen, I've gotta go," Rachel said. "Food's coming. Chin up, eh? And remember what Miss Kasia always said."

"Just go out and have fun."

"No matter what happens."

Juliana hung up. "No matter what happens," Juliana repeated and adjusted the ice pack again. "That's easy for Rachel to say. She doesn't live here."

CHAPTER FOUR

*M*ammi snored, Anna remained silent, Rosina mumbled incoherently in her sleep, and Luki lay as still as an acacia tree. Elisabeth's back ached too much from rolling out so much dough, making it hard for her to get comfortable.

She rolled onto her side and caught a glimpse of the clear night sky. She tried to rub her back to remove the aches and pains from hours of rolling out dough and cutting noodles, but she wasn't having much luck.

Elisabeth rolled onto her back and pulled up her knees, and her back felt momentarily better. She looked out at the stars again and thought back to her afternoon at her aunt's. All the idle gossip that always put other people down. Elisabeth knew she had bad thoughts about people, but she tried hard not to share them with others. Besides, Jesus was watching all of them, wasn't He?

But where does Jesus actually live? she wondered. *Behind the stars? On them?*

Tata's encyclopedia would surely have an answer. It was almost pitch black in the front room, where everyone slept, but she knew the order of the books by heart. She couldn't sleep anyway, so she might as well satisfy her curiosity.

Elisabeth's nervousness grew with each beat of her heart. She couldn't sleep because of her back, but would Mammi let her read? Or would Mammi want Elisabeth to finish up some sewing instead?

But after a day of wedding preparations and endless gossip about others' dresses, shoes, and noses, Elisabeth needed bigger ideas. *If Tata were here, he could answer my questions*, she thought. Since he wasn't here, she would need to find out for herself.

Elisabeth touched the edge of the second row of books, brushed her hand over the first two books on the end and then picked up the third one. It would certainly have something about stars in it. She then tiptoed her way past the table in the middle of the room, touched the back of the now-cooling oven, and followed it to the kitchen door. She retrieved candles from where she'd left them earlier on the washing table and carried them to the back room.

Once she'd lit her candles, she flipped the book open to "Stars." The entry said:

General term for all celestial bodies. One differentiates between stars that emit their own light, planets, comets, moons, or minor planets and shooting stars.

That was it? That was all it could tell her about the lights in the sky? Not even the writers of the encyclopedia knew where Jesus really lived? Or did He maybe not even live in the sky? Feeling disappointed, she pulled the family's Bible down from its shelf in the back room, its weight straining her sore back, and set it on the table. The candles flickered, casting both light and shadow on the thick leather-bound book. But where to start even looking? She glanced at the crucifix above the door. "Jesus," she whispered, "where do I begin?"

The answer came to her like a bolt of lightning. "Begin...of course! The beginning!" she whispered to herself and opened to Genesis, chapter 1:

In the beginning God created the Heaven and the earth. And the earth was without form, and void; and darkness was upon the face of the deep. And the Spirit of God moved upon the face of the waters. And God said, Let there be light: and there was light. And God saw the light, that it was good: and God divided the light from the darkness. And God called the light Day, and the darkness he called Night. And the evening and the morning were the first day. And God said, Let there be a firmament in the midst of the waters, and let it divide the waters from the waters. And God made the firmament, and divided the waters which were under the firmament from the waters which were above the firmament: and it was so. And God called the firmament Heaven. And the evening and the morning were the second day.

Elisabeth read and re-read it, letting the words sink in deeper each time. Her mind was tired and her back hurt, but the more she let the words wash over her, the more certain she became: the sky was indeed Heaven and therefore Jesus' home. She still didn't know *where* in the sky He lived, but He did live up there. She would have to leave it at that for now.

Elisabeth put the Bible back, blew out the candles, and shuffled back to bed. Lying on her side, she again stared out the window into the night sky. Jesus was in the sky and could look down upon them. Did that mean He could see Tata, too? If He could, why didn't He send her a sign that her father was alive and well? Or could Jesus not see him?

If He couldn't, then who was looking out for Tata?

It was mid-morning the next day, and Elisabeth carried a cup of tea in her hands for Mammi, who was hard at work in Tata's workshop. Luki and Anna were at school for the morning, and Rosina was sweeping the kitchen.

Elisabeth still remembered when Tata had added the workshop to the back of the house before Rosina was born.

Before that, he had done his work on the table in the front room where there was more daylight from the large windows. But it meant the family went to sleep with the smells of leather and other people's feet lingering in the room every night. Mammi had said that she wouldn't have space to raise her children or teach the daughters their crafts. She had eventually demanded that Tata build the small attached workshop, and so it had happened with some help from friends as well as craftsmen from Semlak's Gypsy settlement at the edge of the village.

Elisabeth walked along the side of the house, careful not to let Mammi's tea drip over the sides of the cup. With the weather as cold as it was, Mammi needed all the warmth she could get.

When she opened the door, Elisabeth breathed shallowly so as not to be overwhelmed by the odour of feet, leather, and stale air.

"Here, Mammi," she said, setting the cup on the wooden desk that had more nicks and scratches on it than their cutting boards in the kitchen. Tata had made the desk and Elisabeth loved its texture and roughness. Neighbours had donated spare wood they'd had, and he had sawed, hammered, and stained the desk himself. No one threw anything out in Semlak: if you could use it, you did. If you couldn't, you waited until a friend or member of the family asked for it, and you gave it to them.

"Thank you, Lissika," Mammi said.

Mammi had begun making shoes on her own after the New Year, and her first project—just to practice—was a pair of shoes for Anna, who had grown again. Girls' shoes were just a shoe with a strap, easy for Mammi to make.

"Anna's shoes look lovely, Mammi."

Instead of accepting Elisabeth's compliment, Mammi grunted. "The stitching is uneven, and I've had to cut a new strap twice. A waste! Meier Josef will gossip about our family for weeks if he sees these shoes."

Elisabeth needed a moment to think of a good response. "I know I need a new pair, and I would be very happy with the shoes you make, and I'm sure Anna will be, too."

"Don't be stupid, Lissika," Mammi grumbled. "Shoes tell everyone who you are. I can't make your pair until I've made nine pairs for customers, and with this kind of sloppy work, no one will buy from us. Now, get me a small piece of bread and some sausage. I'll be out here a long time."

Elisabeth rushed back around the house and into the kitchen, not bothering to change her boots. She cut a piece of the bread she had baked that morning and a few slices of sausage, put them on a plate, and rushed back to the workshop. Mammi was busy—she didn't have time to wait for a slow daughter.

Once inside the workshop, Elisabeth set the plate down on the desk and surprised herself by yawning.

"Did you not sleep well?" Mammi asked.

Elisabeth shook her head. "My back was sore from yesterday." Before Mammi had a chance to reply, Elisabeth asked if Mammi needed anything else.

"Not for me. But you do need to continue helping with wedding preparations. I also promised we would make a rum roll, yeast *kipfel*, and a pot of goulash."

Elisabeth's eyes popped open. A rum roll? Yeast *kipfel*? Gulasch? Elisabeth had never baked a rum roll before: she wasn't even sure she'd be able to peel the cake off the baking sheet carefully enough to roll it without breaking it! And *kipfel*? Each of the hundred or more triangles of yeasted dough had to be rolled by hand into a crescent shape, brushed with egg yolk, and sprinkled with salt and caraway. The goulash was by far the easiest because it had to sit and simmer on the stove for hours, but it required a lot of meat and peppers and every wife in Semlak had her special way of making it. (Or so they said: Elisabeth could barely tell the difference between them, although this was an observation she kept to herself.)

"You will be helping me, right, Mammi?"

Mammi's eyes flared like bolts of lightning. "Are you saying I haven't taught you well enough to be able to handle this all on your own?"

Elisabeth took a step back. "I-I-I'm sorry," she stammered. "No, not at all, Mammi! I just don't know if I can do it so well that everyone will be proud of our family's contributions to the wedding meal."

Mammi tapped nails into the heels of Anna's shoe, though it sounded louder now to Elisabeth. She didn't mean to anger her mother. Would Jesus forgive her for that, too? She stifled another yawn.

"You've cooked by my side for the past eight years, Elisabeth," Mammi said, her voice stern. "I know you're frightened about peeling the cake off the sheet." Mammi stopped for a moment and made eye contact with her oldest child. "But you are ready to do it by yourself nonetheless."

Elisabeth's heart beat like her mother's hammer had.

"Can I at least try a rum roll on my own once before I bake the real one?"

Mammi slammed the hammer down on her work table. "Are we made of money, Elisabeth? No, of course not! You have time to figure it out. Now go. You have chores to do."

CHAPTER FIVE

*J*uliana's heart fluttered like a young ballet student bourréeing across the floor, faster and faster as she lost her balance and fought to stay *en pointe*.

Only in Juliana's case, she was standing in her boots outside her new studio.

"Come on!" Dad called out from the main entrance. "You're going to be late!" His smile stretched from one side of his face to the other, and Juliana could tell he was excited for her. After laughing at Kitchener's tiny snow ploughs that were nothing more than dump trucks with big shovels on the front, she was finally about to meet her new team.

Juliana nodded, but her feet were frozen in the snow. Her new team would be composed of incredible dancers, but would they like her? Would she have to practise to catch up to them? Could she even improve enough? Bathed in nervousness, she did the only thing she knew how to do: she took a selfie and posted it on social media, captioning it: *At my new studio! #newbie #nervous #dyinginside.* She zipped her phone back into its pouch in her dance bag and ran across the front lawn and to the main entrance. The red sign—Come In! We're Open!—looked so normal and yet so scary. Couldn't they be closed for one more day? Couldn't more snow fall, like right now, and close everything up? She jumped up and down and shook out her hands.

Dad laughed. "I've never seen you this nervous, not even before you head onstage in a finals competition."

"This is new, that—" Juliana's voice cracked and she giggled. "That isn't. I don't know anyone here. I'm scared I won't be good enough."

Dad looked her straight in the eyes. "You will be fine. I didn't drag my daughter across the country just so she could quit when she got cold feet, okay?"

Juliana nodded.

"Good. I had enough of that in my youth. I'm not letting you repeat those mistakes."

Before Juliana could ask Dad what he was talking about, he opened the door and waved her inside. She stepped in to a little foyer with a table to the left that had copies of December's newsletter on it. Juliana picked one up, folded it into a neat rectangle and slid it into her bag, whereas Dad picked up his own copy, folded it into some geometric shape that had no name, and shoved it into his back pocket.

They stamped the snow off their feet, walked to the end of the foyer and then into the waiting room, which had benches along two walls, with coat hooks above. She saw lots of boots but no outerwear. Had people left their boots over the holidays? Where were the jackets? Was she the first one here? That'd make her look like a real nerd. Or really dedicated, which would be better. Then she saw another sign—No shoes past this point. Juliana let out her breath. She was neither the first one here, nor had everyone left their boots behind over the holidays. Her cheeks burned a little as she realized how silly her assumptions were.

"We should follow the rules," Dad said, and both removed their boots.

"Juliana?" An older woman, perhaps in her sixties, with her gray hair styled in an old-fashioned tight perm, came out from behind her desk.

Juliana nodded, her voice locked in her throat.

"I'm Mrs. Laing. We've emailed a few times."

The friendly older woman who looked like she could be anyone's grandmother didn't fit the image Juliana had in her mind of the Mrs. D. Laing who wrote the cold emails. She blushed when she realized she couldn't have been more wrong about this, too.

"Yeah, we did," Juliana said. "Um, where do I go?"

Mrs. Laing smiled like the grandmothers on television who invited their grandchildren inside for a scoop of ice cream after a hot summer's day of outdoor play. Only instead of offering ice cream, Mrs. Laing was inviting Juliana into a new world of dance. "Follow me."

"I'll be back in two hours, okay?" Dad said. "I'm going to pick up some food for tomorrow night. Your mom's family's coming over again."

Part of Juliana wanted to grab Dad by the arm and drag him inside with her, and another part wanted her to act brave and hold up her chin. *You're not a baby anymore!* she admonished herself and waved to Dad.

Mrs. Laing took Juliana down one hallway, pointed out a few music rooms and washrooms, the junior girls' change room, the boys' change room, and then the intermediate girls' change room.

"You're in here. Why don't you leave your bag there and then we'll finish the tour."

Juliana pushed open the heavy door and was greeted by a room with bags all over the benches, and ten or more winter coats on the hooks. She made a mental note to bring her jacket in here next time.

But did this mean she was she the last one? She swallowed. "Am I late?"

Mrs. Laing smiled her kind smile again and shook her

head. "They're just finishing up their acro practice. If I recall, you didn't register for acro this year."

Juliana shook her head. "I've never done it, and Mom and Dad thought it would be too much for me."

"It is very demanding," Mrs. Laing confirmed. "Especially if you haven't done it before."

Juliana's confidence took a nose dive, though it admittedly didn't have very high to dive from. Did that mean all the others in her competition group were human pretzels?

"Come along," Mrs. Laing said, but her urging was gentle, not harsh. She pointed out the senior and adult women's change room, an accessible washroom, a hallway with two small studios for little kids, and then the main hallway with the dance studios.

It seemed to stretch on forever with its high ceilings and white walls.

"There are five studios down that hallway," Mrs. Laing said, "aptly referred to by their numbers."

"Like every other studio, I guess, eh?" Juliana said.

Mrs. Laing responded with her smile. "Get changed, put on your tap shoes, and then go back to Studio 3 in five minutes."

Juliana nodded. She turned around to hurry back and then stopped. "Um, which way?" Her face grew hot and she hadn't even stepped inside a studio yet.

Mrs. Laing's face wrinkled like a raisin as she smiled. She spoke kindly, "You'll be fine, Juliana. Your team is a good team. There's no need to rush. If you walk in one minute late, you walk in one minute late. This is your first day, and I know Miss Denise will be understanding." She pointed Juliana in the right direction.

Was it really this relaxed here? Miss Kasia would positively growl if you walked in a minute late.

Juliana whipped off her warm-up clothes and ripped open her dance bag to find her tap shoes. After a few moments, she began to panic.

"Where...?"

She dumped her bag on the ground and pushed aside hip-hop shoes, jazz shoes, pointe shoes, ballet shoes, toe supplies for her pointe shoes, hair elastics, bobby pins, antiperspirant, leggings, everything. Everything but her tap shoes.

She slapped herself on her forehead. "I left them in the basement!"

Her fingers shaking, she tore open the zipper in her bag with her phone in it. She pressed a button on her phone. "Call Dad" she instructed it. Her hand shook as she waited for her father to answer.

"This is Paul. Sorry I can't talk right now. I'm driving. Leave a message."

Juliana's voice shook. "Dad? Why aren't you picking up? I forgot my tap shoes!"

Realizing yelling at his voicemail was counter-productive, Juliana hung up and dialled home.

"Hello?"

"Opa? Where's Mom?"

"Who is this?"

"Juliana!"

"Oh, of course! You sound like your cousins to my old ears."

Juliana had no time for his grandfathering. "Nice. Where's Mom?"

"Let me think…"

Juliana's heart was ready to break through her rib cage. "She's not home?"

"No, she left to go somewhere, but I don't remember where."

"Okay, I'll try her cell. Thanks—"

"She left it on the table, Yulika. It keeps beeping. Do you know how I turn it off? It annoys me."

Every word Juliana wasn't allowed to use flew into her head and she tried to push them all away. The last thing she needed was for Mrs. Laing to hear her swearing.

"I have to go," Juliana said.

"Is everything okay?"

"I left my tap shoes in the basement. I have to go."

"You'll be fine, Yulika. Don't worry."

"You don't understand! You don't show up to dance class without your shoes!"

"You'll be fine. I can't wait to hear about your first class when you get home." Opa hung up.

Juliana slumped onto the bench. Her first dance class and she didn't have her tap shoes.

"Juliana?" Mrs. Laing knocked on the door. "Is everything okay?"

Juliana could feel tears welling up. You didn't show up for your team unprepared, especially at fourteen. Otherwise it looked like your mom still had to take care of you.

She opened the door. "I left my tap shoes at home." She pressed her hands against her eyes, hoping to keep the tears inside their ducts. Mrs. Laing gently pulled Juliana's hands away from her face.

"It's nothing to be upset up," she said, her voice still kind. "Just tell them they're still in a box somewhere at home."

"But they're not. I have everything all organized." Juliana realized the irony of her statement. "Well, except for my dance bag."

"They don't need to know that. I could show you some of the used shoes, if you'd like. Maybe you could find a pair there?"

The thought of stepping into someone's old, sweaty tap shoes that probably bent in all the wrong places disgusted Juliana. "I'll put on my jazz shoes."

Mrs. Laing placed an arm around her shoulder. "I'll introduce you to everyone. That should make you feel better."

Juliana stood in the room, her feet hidden inside silent jazz shoes. It took all her courage to keep her chin up.

Mrs. Laing laid a hand on her shoulder. "This is Juliana," she said.

Juliana scanned the room and counted fifteen dancers, all dressed in black crop tops, shorts, beige tights, and black tap shoes. How was she going to learn all their names?

The teacher came over to shake Juliana's hand. "Hi, Juliana, I'm Miss Denise. We emailed a few times."

"Hi," she said, her voice quiet. She looked down at her feet. "I'm really sorry—"

"Juliana's tap shoes are still in a box at home," Mrs. Laing interrupted.

Miss Denise smiled. Did everyone here just smile? "Totally understandable," she said. "You'll just be learning today anyways, so you'll be fine."

Juliana nodded and then stared at each of the students. A few gave her a weak smile while others didn't react at all. She could see eyes skip to her feet. Were the others angry at her for forgetting her shoes? For slowing down practice to teach her the routine? For some imperfection on her body? She suddenly worried she might already have sweat marks from all her worrying. No antiperspirant could ever fully keep her from sweating.

"This is Janine," and Miss Denise pointed to a girl with a slicked-back ponytail and properly plucked eyebrows. "This is Isaac…" Miss Denise continued to go around the room, the names blurring into one long one: Jasmin-mackenziebenangelrileysavannahalenadreandlotsmore-shecouldnolongerunderstand.

Juliana wiggled her fingers in a wimpy wave. What else was she supposed to do?

"Sit at the front," Miss Denise instructed her, "and we'll run through the dance a few times so you can see it. Did you bring your notebook?"

Notebook? What notebook? Juliana shook her head. "I have my phone…"

"No, not fast enough and it won't let you draw. Here—" Miss Denise walked over to the computer desk in the studio and grabbed some paper and a pencil. "Make some notes on this, whatever strikes you. We'll fill them in as we go along."

"But I could just record it…"

Miss Denise shook her head. "No recording during class time except four weeks before competition, and even then, only I record it. Nobody wants to risk their imperfections getting online."

Juliana nodded. As she walked to the familiar line of mirrors along the front wall of the studio, she snuck a glance at her armpits. They looked fine. One thing she didn't have to worry about. She sat down, her back against the mirrors.

Everyone walked to their opening positions and Miss Denise hit play on the computer.

The entire group began a simultaneous opening sequence, tapping in unison. Juliana scrambled to scribble steps and counts down, but there was no way she could keep up.

Miss Denise noticed. "Just write down what you can," she yelled over the music. "You won't get everything."

Juliana nodded, but she didn't really understand what Miss Denise meant. She'd never taken notes before about a dance she'd never learned. Sure, when she'd broken her wrist and sprained her ankle a couple of years ago, she wrote down errors and corrections, but she had already learned her own dances that year.

The dancers kicked, turned, and tapped in unison like a New York City stage revue chorus. Some arms were out of place, and sometimes heads were at different angles, but otherwise things looked pretty together.

By the time the dance was over three minutes later, Juliana realized she hadn't written anything down. No shoes and no notes. Could this get any worse?

"What did you think?" Miss Denise asked.

It could get worse. What was Juliana supposed to say? That she didn't think she could meet them at their level? That there was no way she'd be as good as them? Maybe forgetting her shoes had been a good thing: that way they'd never know how bad she really was.

"Um, I really liked it," was all she could think of to say.

"What errors did you notice?"

Juliana stared at everyone. Miss Kasia said that if you were going to point out someone's mistake, you'd better perform that step better than they did, otherwise you'd look like a stuck-up snob from some TV dance show. Juliana didn't know if she could live up to any corrections she was about to give. But as all eyes were glued to her, she knew she had to say something.

"I found sometimes the arms weren't always in line."

Miss Denise nodded and then looked at the group. "See? It's not just me."

To Juliana's surprise, everyone nodded. No looks of anger flew in her direction, and several even smiled.

"Let's try it again," Miss Denise said.

"WHY DIDN'T YOU ANSWER YOUR PHONE!" JULIANA SHOUTED at Dad.

"Because I'd forgotten it in the car!" Dad yelled back. "*You* forgot to pack your shoes. Why are you yelling at me?"

"Don't know you how embarrassed I was?"

Dad paused for a moment, took a deep breath, and visibly tried to calm himself down. "I can imagine it would be like me showing up to my new employer without my truck driver's license," he said. "So, yes, I do get it, Juliana. But I wouldn't pick up the phone and start yelling at your mother for not reminding me!"

Juliana's whole body was filled with anger. "I can't show up without my shoes and just expect them to be okay with it!"

"You'll get a second chance to prove yourself!"

"A second chance? You really don't get it, do you, Dad?"

"What? Did they yell at you? Make you do embarrassing initiation games? Kick you out and tell you to never come back?"

"Well, no."

"Then they were fine with it and they're giving you a second chance. For once in your life, be grateful for something. Please!"

"That's not what they were thinking!"

"Oh, so you can read thoughts now, can you?"

Juliana crossed her arms. "These things may not be important to adults, but they're absolutely important to teens!"

Dad banged on the steering wheel. "I've already told you that I understand, Juliana! You're the one who needs to grow up here and take responsibility for your actions! They're obviously giving you a second chance!"

Juliana couldn't wait to get home and talk to Rachel. She'd at least understand.

CHAPTER SIX

A week had passed, and Anna and Elisabeth had just picked up their sewing bags at home, after church, and now stood under the overhang outside Konrad-Bátschi and Margarethe-Néni's house. Elisabeth knocked. Today's task would be embroidering handkerchiefs for the bridesmaids.

The door opened, and Eva, Cousin Georg's wife, stood there, smiling from ear to ear. "Lissika! Little Anna! It's so wonderful to see you both!"

They exchanged kisses on each other's cheeks, and Elisabeth wondered how often she'd have to endure being greeted by members of this family as though they hadn't seen each other in months.

"Come in, let me take your shawls!"

Elisabeth and Anna removed their winter shawls and then their mittens.

"May I?" Anna asked, pointing to the table next to the stove.

Eva gave her an exaggerated expression of disappointment, the kind an adult gives a three-year-old. "Boys again?"

Anna's temples twitched and Elisabeth knew her sister was annoyed. She detested being treated as though she was as young as Rosina. Elisabeth had to speak up but before she could say anything, Gretche interrupted.

"Lissika! Anna! Thank you for coming! I already have tea in the front room for us. The men have left for a while, so we'll be all alone, just like the last time!"

And just like last time, Elisabeth tried not to roll her eyes. She didn't want to spend time gossiping about whatever Meier Josef had been gossiping about at church that day. As far as Elisabeth was concerned, if she had time away from household chores, she'd rather be reading than listening to everyone talk about everyone else. But duty was duty, and as a cousin to the bride, she had to help.

At least this time she wouldn't go home with a sore back.

The front room in Konrad-Bátschi's home was similar to Elisabeth's: a wooden, handmade table that could seat eight or maybe ten stood in the middle, and beds were spread out along the room's walls. In between the two large windows stood a wooden bench with a back, furniture that had been passed down for several generations in the family. To the left of the door was the back of the lime-painted brick oven, which heated the room comfortably. When Elisabeth and Anna were shown in, they nodded hello to Margarethe-Néni and Susi, who smiled back, and then took their seats at the table, between Gretche and Eva. It was only family today, which relieved Elisabeth of the agony of listening to a dozen women gossip.

"Have you heard from Lukas-Bátschi yet?" Eva asked, referring to Elisabeth's and Anna's father. But the question surprised Elisabeth: Eva could have begun their conversation with a happier topic, couldn't she?

"No," Elisabeth replied. "Not yet."

Eva's face turned upside down. "I'm so sorry. I'm certain he's fine."

"I hope so. It's been almost two months. We should have heard from him by now."

Eva nodded, her face openly sad. "It must be hard not know how he's faring."

Elisabeth heard a little sniffle from Anna and knew she had to change the topic. That Eva would purposely begin with such an upsetting subject angered Elisabeth: Eva was a woman now. She should know better.

"How are wedding plans coming along?" Elisabeth asked, trying her best to keep her tone polite.

Margarethe-Néni smiled. "We have so many people

helping us that we are much farther along by now than we were with Georg's wedding last year."

"That's wonderful to hear," Elisabeth replied, not sure if she really meant it. But she knew that Margarethe-Néni was only telling half the truth herself: part of the reason for the delays in Georg's wedding were his tremors, during which he would press himself into a corner in the room and fight his body to stop shaking, a difficult and embarrassing habit that had begun after the war. Eva almost hadn't married him but, according to Mammi, she had after she was reminded of the benefits of the union. At the very least, it had meant that Eva's family could pay less of a dowry to Georg's family. Elisabeth hoped that, whoever her husband would be, he would be in good health and not request much of her family. With only one boy and three girls to marry off, Tata and Mammi could find the marriage of their children very expensive.

"May I ask how Georg is doing?" Elisabeth said. "I only see him in church, but he seems to be doing better."

"Thank you," Eva said. "Yes, God has been shining his blessings down on him."

"That's nice to hear, isn't it, Anna?" Elisabeth said, and her sister nodded. Anna rarely said a word outside the home, and Elisabeth felt that it was part of her duty in helping raise her siblings that she needed to teach shy Anna how to converse. After all, no man would want a silent wife.

THE CLOCK CHIMED THREE, AND IT WAS NEARLY TIME TO leave: Elisabeth needed to cook supper. She looked over to Anna's handiwork to see how far she'd come. Anna had chosen a simple rose pattern for her handkerchief: two roses in each corner, their petals stitched in red thread and their leaves and stem in green. Seven of the eight roses were already finished, and Elisabeth knew Mammi would certainly be upset if her daughters left without finishing.

"That looks lovely," Elisabeth said, and Anna beamed. The other women glanced over at the young girl's work and nodded in approval.

"You'll make a fine wife someday if you keep up with that," said Margarethe-Néni. "And speak a little more. We've hardly heard you say a thing these past several hours."

Anna's temples twitched, but no one seemed to notice. The conversation simply continued about others in the village. Elisabeth had had to stifle yawns several times to prevent herself from drifting off to sleep, stabbing herself with her needle, or thinking about Tata. Why hadn't she heard from him yet? She glanced up at the crucifix that hung over the doorway. Was Tata truly so far away that not even Jesus could see him? Why else wouldn't Jesus give Elisabeth a sign that he was well? She was trying so hard to be a pious girl—surely some good must come of her efforts?

"Anna, finish up," she said to her sister. "We should go: I need to start supper shortly."

She headed through the kitchen into the back room to retrieve their shawls. As she returned, Georg entered through the house door. His short hair was neatly trimmed, his face shaven clean, and his broad chest and thick arms showed no signs of feebleness. He removed his hat and nodded.

"Hello, Elisabeth," he said, though without a smile.

The creases in his face made him look older than he was. If he had been anyone else, Elisabeth would have taken his still face to mean something rude, and indeed, many in the village did view him that way. His shaking, his unfriendly greetings, his quiet demeanour—all these things often embarrassed his family. But he was a tradesman: he would take over his father's blacksmith shop someday, so that—and only that—gave him respect, because there were few tradesmen among the German Lutherans.

"I'm here to pick up Eva to go visit her family."

"We're almost finished, I believe," Elisabeth answered, frozen in her spot.

Georg removed his boots without saying another word, walked into the front room, and nodded to everyone around the table.

"Hello, Georg," Eva said, beaming, but even to such a happy welcome he just nodded and left the room. Elisabeth saw Margarethe-Néni's flash of anger once Georg turned around, while Eva's face fell. Elisabeth wondered if this happened all the time. To Elisabeth's relief, Anna was just tying off her threads.

Elisabeth hung the shawls over the back of a chair and smoothed out her handkerchief on the table: she had two blue birds in each corner, joined by a chain of leaves that travelled along each edge. For an extra blessing, she had embroidered a little star on top of each pair of birds. She had begun the handkerchief earlier in the week, so she finished it today.

"Elisabeth, you truly have a gift from God," Margarethe-Néni said and thanked her.

"I can do one more at home if you'd like," Elisabeth offered. It wasn't as enjoyable as the drawing she loved to do, but it would give her a break from her chores without causing Mammi to complain. Margarethe-Néni happily accepted the offer and handed her another cotton square. Elisabeth and Anna collected their bags and shawls and the others followed them, congregating at the house door, in the kitchen. Georg was sitting at the table, puffing on a cigarette. Judging by his unfocused eyes, he was lost in thought.

"Georg," Eva said, "your cousins are leaving."

Georg nodded to both girls but otherwise said nothing.

Elisabeth and Anna wrapped their shawls around their shoulders, and Gretche reached around Anna to the table beside the oven to pass Anna her red mittens.

"No," Georg said, shaking his head. His cigarette dropped onto the floor and Georg jumped up from his chair, his eyes fixed on the mittens.

"Georg," Eva said, her voice polite but stern. "I just told your cousins that you're doing better. Stop this."

Still staring at the mittens, he wrapped his arms around himself, as though he was trying to stop his body from shaking.

"Don't shoot!" he yelled.

Realizing the mittens had somehow caused his change, Elisabeth turned Anna around, said a hurried round of goodbyes herself, and rushed out.

"No!" she could hear Georg call from inside. "Leave him!"

The girls walked around to the front of the house, where Elisabeth stopped in her tracks as she saw Margarethe-Néni slap Georg in the face. "Stop embarrassing our family!" she screamed, her voice carrying through the several panes of windows. She saw Georg collapse in the doorway.

Anna's eyes and mouth were wide open, and Elisabeth didn't know what to tell her. "We should go," she said and tried to push Anna along.

"But he needs help," Anna replied.

"He has family. They will help him." She looked up to the sky. Jesus saw this, did He not? He must have. If the two girls had seen Georg, then Jesus must have, too. "Jesus will help Georg, too, when He feels it's right."

"Shouldn't Jesus help him right now? Margarethe-Néni isn't."

Elisabeth didn't have an answer.

Anna turned around and began heading back to their aunt's house.

"No," Elisabeth said. "It's none of our business, Anna."

Her younger sister's eyes began to moisten. "But he's hurting."

Elisabeth turned Anna around, back to the sidewalk, and pushed her along. "Jesus will find a way to help him. We can help by praying for him."

ELISABETH HAD MANAGED TO CALM ANNA DOWN BY THE TIME they got home, even though her own mind swirled in confusion. She remembered Gretche and Susi complaining all the time about their older brother when they were all younger: Georg would pull their hair or poke them in the ear with a wet finger when no one was looking. He loved playing a *storrnickel* at Christmas and frightening all the younger children at every house he visited. Elisabeth remembered those years all too well. Most of her childhood was spent running out of the room every time Georg entered it.

But the more time he had spent with his father in the workshop, the less time he had had to bother his family. With the strength of a mule and the aim of a hummingbird, Georg had become a respected blacksmith well before he married his first wife. He carried pride in his chest wherever he walked, acting more and more like a man and not a bothersome brother. Georg could wield a hammer to make almost anything: horseshoes, hoops for wine barrels, even occasionally ploughs and parts for ploughs.

And now he trembled at the sight of red mittens.

Once both sisters were inside their own house and had removed their shawls and boots, Elisabeth helped herself to a glass of water from the jug that sat next to the washing basin. Luki was in the front room playing with a rubber ball, trying to knock over some dried corn cobs that had been cut in half so they would stand. Sitting at the table, Rosina stuck out her tongue in concentration as she tried to crochet the first row after her chain. Elisabeth remembered having difficulty with those first few rows when she was young: sticking the hook through those often tight loops was frustrating. It was also partly why she had taken to drawing: she didn't have to coordinate her hands so much. Anna sat down next to her sister and resumed a scarf she was crocheting for herself.

Mammi, too, sat at the table, though she was knitting a sock while reading the Bible.

"Mammi?" Elisabeth sat down and pulled out her embroidery ring.

"Mmm," Mammi replied, not looking up from her reading.

Elisabeth separated the ring into its inner and outer parts, placed the fresh square of cotton from Margarethe-Néni in it, closed the outer ring on top, and tightened the screw. "I saw Cousin Georg at Margarethe-Néni's today."

"Couldn't step outside his own home again?"

Elisabeth tried to ignore the tone in Mammi's voice. "He had actually just returned to get Eva so they could visit her family."

"I see." Mammi said no more, her mind clearly focused on knitting and reading instead of talking with her daughter.

Elisabeth persisted. "Why is he like that?"

Mammi's face didn't move when she answered, and her eyes still followed the words in the Bible. "He has weak nerves, Elisabeth, you know that."

Mammi clearly didn't want to be disturbed, but Elisabeth couldn't let it rest.

"But Eva said today that he was doing better, and all it took was Anna's red mittens to..." She didn't know how to describe what she'd seen.

"He fell onto the floor like a sack of potatoes again, did he?"

Elisabeth nodded.

"He obviously isn't the man everyone thought he was, and the war proved that. He's lucky he found a second wife."

Elisabeth threaded some green into her needle and took a moment to look up at Jesus.

Why can't You help him? she silently asked.

ELISABETH SAT IN THE BACK ROOM, SEVERAL CANDLES LIT, and her book of drawings open to the next page. The rest of the family lay in bed, fast asleep. She could not get Georg out of her mind, the way he had shaken and panicked at the sight of a pair of mittens. The memory kept pounding against her skull like a blacksmith's hammer.

And then Mammi's comment: "He fell onto the floor like a sack of potatoes again, did he?"

Wouldn't Georg stop if he could? Or was this God's punishment for the way Georg had behaved to his family and other children when they were all younger? The snowballs Anna had to deal with from other school kids paled in comparison to the teasing, hair-pulling, and private insults Georg would throw his sisters' way and the fights he would start with his lame brother. She even vaguely recalled him telling her a long time ago that they'd never have money because Tata hadn't been the one to inherit his father's blacksmithing shop.

"But in truth," Elisabeth whispered, "Tata never wanted it. He hated the heat." That was of course something that was simply not said. Tata would never have wanted to insult his father or his father's memory.

But if Georg couldn't shake off these tremors, how terrible must it be to have them? To be trapped in a body that trembled of its own will? At the sight of a simple pair of handmade, woollen mittens?

Ideas flew through Elisabeth's mind and she fervently began with an outline: Georg's hands pulling the mittens off Anna's. Elisabeth believed Georg would've wanted to do that, to rid himself of whatever the red mittens reminded him of. At the same time, Elisabeth believed that something inside him was screaming for help; it just didn't know what to do. Georg was a man who had never asked for help, but how could one be caged in such a body that didn't respond to one's own commands?

She began to shade in his hands.

But how could anyone enter inside such a mind to drive out the affliction? Or would it take a blessing from Jesus to do that? And if so, why wasn't Jesus giving Georg His blessing?

CHAPTER SEVEN

On her bed, Juliana fumbled several times as she tried to text Rachel.

R u there? Need to talk!

"You have to answer!" Juliana yelled at her phone. "Rachel, where are you?"

"Yulika?" Opa asked from outside her room. "Are you all right?" Again he came in without knocking.

Juliana shook her head. "I had a horrible day at the studio."

Opa rubbed the top of his bald head. "Because of your dance shoes?"

"Yeah. And Rachel's not even answering my calls or texts!"

"But how can that make you this upset?"

Juliana threw her phone on her bed and looked up at

him. "I forgot my dance shoes. It was a total embarrassment!"

"Yulika, there are much worse things in the world to be upset about."

Another adult who didn't empathize.

"It's just not something you do when you start with a new dance team," Juliana said. "And then I couldn't get hold of Dad to get them for me. They're going to think I don't care!"

"I can see that you do care, though," he said, "so I think your friends could, too."

He gestured to the chair, and Juliana nodded. He sat down, only to surprise himself as it tipped back a few inches.

"Are you okay?" Juliana asked.

Opa laughed. "You can even hurt yourself in chairs these days."

Juliana got off her bed and adjusted the chair so it would stay still.

"Let me tell you a story," he said.

Inwardly, Juliana rolled her eyes: she really wasn't in the mood for a story right now. And if Rachel texted her back, Juliana would have to wait to reply until Opa finished. "Opa, can you tell me later? I'm hoping Rachel calls me."

"No. Your family comes first, your friend can wait," he replied, taking Juliana somewhat aback with his directness. He didn't wait for any further response from her and began. "Mammi had a cousin," Opa began. "Georg. *He* didn't care."

Juliana couldn't figure out if this story was serious or if Opa was setting her up for a joke. If a joke, it'd be short at least.

"The only reason people respected him was because he was a blacksmith."

Rats. His tone told her this wasn't going to be a joke. She really didn't want a lecture about not caring right now. She knew what it meant to arrive to dance on time and prepared and she needed to be accepted into this team. She loved what the studio had to offer, and now that she'd met Mrs. Laing and Miss Denise, she knew it was where she needed to be. She had wanted to make a good first impression and instead she had screwed up big time! Why could no one understand that? The last thing she needed was to hear about some ancient relative who didn't feel like walking to school, uphill both ways.

But Opa had her cornered. She tucked her knees into her chest and listened. What else was she going to do?

Opa continued. "Almost every day, after Georg worked only a few hours in his blacksmith shop, he'd stop working. Just like that. He didn't care enough about his wife and family to look after them. To *work* so he could look after them. And everyone knew it. He wasn't a man, Yulika. Men look after their families, and Georg did not."

Juliana really had no interest in lessons from the past.

All she wanted was to talk to someone who understood what she was going through and how important this was. Opa was a wonderful person, but now was a really bad time. She sighed in a way that suggested she was already bored, hoping he would get the message.

He didn't.

"You act like the world is falling apart because you forgot your shoes once. Georg forgot his wife and children, his family, every day. He was an embarrassment to his family."

Juliana had to admit that that did sound bad. But a nagging feeling told her there was more to this story. "Why was he like that?"

"He was fine before the war. When he came back, he was weak. The whole congregation disliked him because he didn't care about his wife and five children." Opa paused, lost in thought. He shook his head again. "Mammi told me years later that none of his children turned out to be good people. The way he acted didn't teach his children how to behave."

"What? What do you mean?"

Opa waved his hand in the air, dismissing her question. "It doesn't matter. I don't talk to them. They're somewhere in Germany now. Too expensive to call, and Mammi said they're not nice people."

Juliana mulled the story over in her mind. A man goes

to war, returns, and changes. "Wait. You're complaining about him because he had PTSD?"

"I don't know anything about the new words you kids use these days." He shook his finger at her. It was a friendly shaking, but a shaking nonetheless. "If you want to know what not caring was, Yulika, it was Georg. Forgetting your shoes once doesn't mean you don't care. Forgetting your family everyday does."

Juliana didn't know how to respond. She knew Opa meant well: he was trying to comfort her, probably trying to connect with her, and yet he was talking about how an entire church had turned its back on a man who'd served in the war. She had to explain. Maybe Opa just didn't know.

"Opa, PTSD is post-traumatic stress disorder. It means that your mind can't handle when you've gone through something really painful and traumatic. It sounds like your mother's cousin had that."

Opa's eyes narrowed. "It doesn't matter what you call it. If you can't provide for your family, you're not a man, and that's how you'll be remembered. There were several other men in Semlak who were fine after the war, including Mammi's father. Georg shouldn't have come back. It would've been easier for everyone that way."

With that, he stood up and left. Juliana watched him go, her jaw practically on the bed. Only once she could hear his steps going down the stairs did she dare to move, one limb at a time, until she was standing. She walked over to her door and closed it, catching a glance of herself in her full-length mirror.

"A man is traumatized by war and he 'doesn't care'?" she said aloud.

Was this dementia? Saying unreasonable things like that? Or was that really her grandfather? But how could he be so uncaring? At the same time, though, his story wasn't some jumbled-up string of sentences. Opa wasn't like those commercials about dementia Juliana had seen when she and Mom had watched sitcoms together back in Calgary, commercials where an old man had left lemons all around the kitchen. And Opa was certainly a lot more mobile than old people who needed bathtubs with doors or used lifts that took them up and down flights of stairs.

No, she was certain: those really were his thoughts. Not only had Dad disappointed her today, but Opa now, too.

JULIANA HAD EVENTUALLY FALLEN ASLEEP AFTER WAITING TO hear from Rachel for at least a half hour. Her eyes just opening now, she checked the time on her phone. Supper wouldn't be for a while. Feeling groggy, Juliana packed her tap shoes to make sure she wouldn't forget them for her next practice: she was not going to show up tomorrow, New Year's Eve day, without her shoes again. If her new team was giving her a second chance, she didn't want to screw it up.

After she zipped up her bag, she threw it next to her door, dropped back on to her bed, grabbed her phone, and logged into a social media account. "You really need some friends, Juliana," she said to herself. "You can't change the past, but you can talk to your friends." She saw that several of them had posted pictures from Christmas dance practice. She clicked on hearts, left a few notes to some friends, and then began typing a new status: *Survived 1st day at new studio.* Normally, she'd add another detail or two, maybe describe how awesome it was, or how great she looked... but she had nothing good to write there. "Survived" described exactly how she felt.

"Juliana!" Mom called from the kitchen. "I need your help!"

Juliana sighed. She just needed a few minutes alone to touch base with her friends, so she ignored Mom.

Miss Denise was really cool, and thinking about Mrs. Laing made Juliana smile. She could write, *Felt warm hearts all around* ♥♥♥. But would her old friends back in Calgary think she liked the new studio better? "Okay, what about 'Great place, miss the old one, though?'" she asked out loud. But if anyone from the new studio was looking for her and saw her post, would they think she preferred her old one? She wanted to let her friends know how she was doing, but she couldn't figure out what to write so she wouldn't make anyone angry or make herself look dumb.

"Juliana!"

"Give me a minute!" Juliana shouted back.

"Now!" her mother replied.

"I said, give me a minute!"

Footsteps immediately pounded down the hallway to her room and Dad stormed in. "That is not how you talk to your mother," he said, his arms crossed. "She asked for your help, and you have nothing to do right now."

Juliana didn't need this, not after how the rest of the day had gone. "Why can't you help her? You have nothing to do!" Why was it always that adults were happy to point fingers at kids, but the same rules didn't apply to them?

"Because I do a lot to help out your mom already. I've cleaned out that entire garage, unpacked boxes, driven you to dance—"

"And weren't available on your phone?" Juliana wasn't going to let this rest. Dad could've helped Mom in the kitchen for the few minutes she needed if it was that important.

"You forgot your shoes, young lady, not me."

"You're my dad! You're supposed to help me!"

"And your mom is trying to help you right now by teaching you how to cook!"

Juliana's parents always found a way to twist things

around so problems were her fault. She grunted. "That only helps her."

"Excuse me?" Dad said, pretending not to have heard what she had said.

"You heard me. My helping her cook only helps her."

Dad's face began to turn red. "Do you have any idea how lucky you are to have two parents who want to teach you how to be an adult?"

Juliana fingered through the icons on her phone, more just to annoy Dad than anything else. There was no way she was going to accept being spoken to like this, especially not today. Dad had the audacity to yell at her for how she spoke to Mom, when Mom was the one who had no patience? What gave him that right? She had looked like a loser to her new dance team, then Opa had lectured her about not caring, and now this?

"Nope," she replied, trying to annoy Dad even more.

Dad threw his hands up in the air. "No, of course you don't, because you have two parents."

"Excuse me?" Juliana said. "I have two parents? I've seen the two of you more these past two weeks than I have in my entire life! I don't have parents! I have two adults who spend so much time at work they feel like ghosts to me! If you call that parenting, then I have no idea what manual you read!"

The air in the room buzzed like a swarm of angry wasps.

Dad sighed his trying-to-calm-down sigh, the one that hissed through his nose. "I am not getting into an argument with you about this. One day you're going to move out, and I don't care if you think that's tomorrow or in ten years, but you have to learn how to look after yourself. Trust me, it's not easy learning all that on your own."

"What would you know about that? I'm the one left here by myself all the time!"

He sighed loudly again, sat down in her desk chair, rested his elbows on his knees, and leaned forward.

Another lecture, Juliana thought. *Do I get a loyalty reward when I've heard ten?*

But then she noticed something different about Dad: it was as though a dark cloud had settled over him. She'd never gotten this feeling from him before, but she didn't know if it was because she'd just never been around to see it or because he'd never felt it.

"I'm going to keep this short," he said, "because I know you hate these lectures. There's a reason I hardly speak about my family, Juliana, and it's because I barely had one."

Dad stared at the floor as he spoke. "I didn't always make the best choices because my parents were hardly part of my life. My dad was always at work, trying to support me, and my mother...let's just say she wasn't a part of my life at all."

Juliana's eyes popped out of her head. "I—I'm sorry," she whispered. "I had no idea."

Dad waved her apology away, suggesting though that it wasn't necessary, not that he was ignoring it. He continued. "I got into trucking, because my only other option coming out of high school that offered any kind of future was the military."

He paused, and Juliana had collected herself enough now that she knew not to say anything. After a minute of silence, he spoke again.

"When your mother and I decided to have you, I was faced with two choices: find a local job that would pay less but keep me home or keep doing what I do so you could have all the opportunities you wanted in life. Your mom had had those opportunities. She couldn't imagine a life without them and I wished I'd had a life with them. So we decided that my staying in trucking was the better option."

Dad stopped and looked up again. Juliana thought he wanted to say more, and she was ready to listen. It was as though a rope had formed between them, and if Juliana grabbed hold and her father did the same, then they might create a new connection, one that couldn't be cut.

The idea frightened her. She was a teenager: teens didn't have connections to their parents like babies did. At the same time, though, something was missing inside Juliana and that magical rope could—somehow—replace that emptiness. The best she could do now, she believed, was to ask a question to show she was interested in hearing more, that she was willing to listen.

"Why wasn't your mother around?"

Just then, Mom called from the kitchen.

"Are you coming?"

"Just a moment," Dad replied.

"All right," Mom called, "but the lettuce isn't being washed by itself!"

Juliana sighed and rolled her eyes. "Do I have to wash lettuce?"

She clapped her hand over her mouth and the dark cloud that hovered over Dad turned into a hurricane.

"Did you not hear a word I just said? How ungrateful can you be?"

Juliana wished she could disappear into her phone and slide away deep into the Internet. Her words had come out before she could cut them off and now they had cut that rope.

Dad stood up. "You have no idea how good you have it!" He stormed out of her room.

"I'm sorry," she managed to say, although he was too far down the hallway to hear it.

CHAPTER EIGHT

"He's still burning, Mammi." Elisabeth touched Luki's forehead.

Mammi wiped her hands on her apron even though she wasn't cooking, a signal to Elisabeth that her mother was scared.

Luki had been sent home from school that morning, the sixteenth child since last week. By the time he'd reached the house, his face was whiter than the snow outside, and he could barely walk. It had been a fight just to get a few spoonfuls of chicken broth into him.

"Leave him covered up—he needs to sweat it out. People need new shoes for the wedding. Get me only if it's important." With that, Mammi headed back out to the workshop.

Important? Luki was sweating without blankets on him and he seemed to be fading in and out of awareness. If that wasn't important, what was?

Elisabeth got Luki a glass of water and gave him a few sips with a spoon.

"I'm really hot," he complained, sweat dripping down his temples. His little body convulsed as he coughed, his chest gurgling like rough waters in the Marosch River.

"Then let's get a sleeping gown on you. I don't think it's good to leave your clothes on. Can you get changed?"

Luki rocked his head slowly from side to side, and Elisabeth realized she'd have to do it. She wiped her hands on her apron, took a deep breath, and then rolled back the blanket.

"Do what you can to undress. I'll get you your nightgown."

It took some juggling and jostling, contorting and coughing, but between the two of them, they got Luki changed. Elisabeth gave him more water on the spoon, washed down his forehead, and covered him back up.

"Let me get you a little bread."

"I'm not hungry," Luki groaned.

"But you need something in you to give you strength."

Luki shook his head. His eyes closed and then opened, closed and then opened. It seemed pointless to Elisabeth to force him to do anything right now.

"Rest," she told him. "See if you can get some sleep."

Luki didn't say another word. His eyes closed and his head tipped to the side.

Elisabeth gently covered him with the blanket and then knelt beside him, placed her elbows on the bed, and clasped her hands together in prayer. She recited the first one that came to her for this kind of situation, though she had to change it a little.

Now Luki lays himself down to sleep.
I pray the Lord his soul to keep.
If he should die before he wakes,
I pray the Lord his soul to take.

Tears ran down her cheeks. There wasn't a winter that would go by without children dying from fevers. This was the only time where Elisabeth was glad that the church bells were gone, melted into ammunition for the war. It meant she couldn't hear the familiar patterns of ringing that announced almost daily that a funeral for a child was about to begin.

If Luki died, would his soul fly with angels to Heaven, in the sky? Elisabeth shook the thought out of her head. Why would God threaten to take Luki? Her little brother had done nothing wrong—his antics, his arguments, they were all because he was a boy. Certainly God wouldn't take away a person because of how He created him, would He?

The house door in the kitchen opened and shut. Elisabeth could tell by the footsteps that it was Mammi. She wiped her eyes and stood up.

Mammi's usually harsh lines in her face softened when she saw Elisabeth's tears.

"Jesus told me to come inside," she whispered. "I know we are thinking the same thing, but we must be strong. You have two sisters and now your mother who need you: the animals must be cared for so we have meat. Meals must be cooked, because you need strength to keep caring for your brother, and I, to keep making shoes. If we fail in our responsibilities, then your brother will die and no one will buy shoes from us, which means we will soon run out of money to pay for whatever we cannot make ourselves. This is our life, Elisabeth. It is hard, but it brings us happiness: we have God, Jesus, our family, our friends, and our purpose in life. We need very little, but we must hold on to what little we have."

Elisabeth's situation seemed hopeless to her now. How was she supposed to take care of Luki, help Anna with her homework, keep Rosina occupied, cook supper, embroider that handkerchief, iron, figure out that rum roll for the wedding...? Mammi was right, but Elisabeth still couldn't figure out how to do it all.

"He's resting for now," Mammi said. "Get to work. Our family needs you." She gave Elisabeth a nod and retreated to the family's workshop.

Elisabeth stifled a yawn. She had been up until at least two o'clock drawing, trying to get that image of Georg's hands on Anna's mittens out of her mind and onto paper where she could see it. She had hoped to sleep while Luki was sleeping, even if only for a few minutes, before getting on with her chores. But that most certainly wouldn't happen now. Jesus was watching.

Luki coughed again, his body shaking. His eyes opened. "I'm hot…"

Elisabeth gave him a few more sips of water from the spoon. He coughed a few more times, and then drifted off again.

ELISABETH HAD A POT OF SOUP ON THE STOVE AND ONE OF Anna's school dresses ready to iron on the kitchen table. She grabbed a cloth to protect her hand as she opened the hot oven door. With her other hand, she used a poker to push the coals to the side. She shoved in corn stalks, spread them out, and closed the oven door. She'd put the chicken in the oven in the next hour or so.

"Anna! Can you get me more cornstalks?"

Anna's quiet shuffle from the back room to the kitchen was the only answer Elisabeth got.

"You could at least say you heard me," Elisabeth said.

Anna put on her boots and headed outside into the

blistering cold. "I heard you!" she yelled as the door closed behind her.

Elisabeth wiped her brow with her forearm. Was the entire afternoon going to be like this? She quickly scrubbed two carrots clean.

"Rosina!" she called to her younger sister, who was also sitting in the back room. "Can you chop these carrots?"

"I'm busy stiching!"

Elisabeth crossed her arms and stomped over to her sister, who was casting her first row of stitches onto a knitting needle.

"You mean 'knitting,' and you've hardly knit a thing."

"I'm six!"

"Rosina, I need your help in the kitchen."

"And I want to knit Luki a blanket so he can get better!"

"With any luck, you'll be done by your own wedding."

Rosina's lips began to quiver as her mouth started its slow descent to turn upside down.

Elisabeth threw up her hands. "I'm sorry! I didn't mean to hurt your feelings! We have so much to do here and I need your help!"

Rosina followed Elisabeth to the kitchen, although not happily.

"Peel these two carrots," Elisabeth said, trying to calm her voice, "and let me know when you're done. I'll cut them in half so chopping is easier for you."

Rosina did as she was told, but with a big frown on her face.

Next on Elisabeth's list was to boil some water for linden tea for Luki. Anna stomped back inside just then with cornstalks under her arm and handed them to Elisabeth, who gave her sister a pot in return.

"What if the well's frozen?" Anna asked.

"The well is thirty feet down!" Elisabeth said. "The water will be fine!"

Anna stamped her foot. "Stop yelling at me. You're not Mammi!"

Elisabeth rolled her eyes. "I know that! But I still need water to make Luki tea!"

"Fine!" Anna stomped back out of the house with the pot.

Elisabeth looked up to the crucifix hanging over the door to the front room. "Since you're watching over us, can you please protect Luki? And if you find some time, can you also help me a little?"

"The carrots are ready!"

Elisabeth saw Rosina kneeling on a chair at the kitchen table with a knife in her hands. The peels lay all over the table's surface instead of in the slop pail. Elisabeth let out an exasperated sigh. She split the carrots lengthwise down the centre and then let Rosina continue chopping while she cleaned up the peels.

"All right. What's next?" she asked herself. She'd been so wrapped up in the fights with her sisters that she'd completely forgotten her list of chores. She wiped her hands on her apron. She had to iron, stir the soup simmering on the stove, get the chicken in the oven...but not just yet...first she had to make Luki a tea.

Luki.

She rushed into the front room to check on him. He hadn't coughed—or opened his eyes—in a couple of hours. Elisabeth sat down beside him on the bed.

His forehead still burned, but he'd stopped sweating. His face looked like that of a porcelain doll: his cheeks were bright red, his eyelids mauve, and his lips almost burgundy. But he was breathing.

The bed was so comfortable and warm. Elisabeth yawned.

Only a few minutes' sleep...that's all she would need to freshen up a little. Just a few minutes...

"Elisabeth Schuhmacher!"

Elisabeth jumped out of Luki's bed. Only then did she hear Rosina crying and see Mammi standing in the doorway, her face red.

"Rosina cut herself, the soup has boiled all over the

stove, the chicken should have gone in the oven a half-hour ago, and Luki still doesn't have his tea!"

Elisabeth's heart fell to the floor. She saw that Luki was also awake from all the noise. "I'm...I'm sorry," she stammered.

"Why are you sleeping?" Mammi screamed at her. "Your family needs you and you're in bed, sleeping like a lazy drunk from the city!"

Tears streamed down Elisabeth's face.

Mammi touched her forehead. "You're not feverish. Why in God's name are you sleeping?"

"I'm just tired," she said, wiping her eyes. She wondered if Jesus had maybe turned His attention to another family.

Mammi looked her up and down and then drilled her gaze into Elisabeth. "No, you're not 'just tired.'" Her gaze jumped to the rows of books in the room. "Tata always leaves those perfectly lined up. But now one of them is sticking out, as though...as though someone put it back at night." Mammi stormed through the kitchen and into the back room and returned holding a few candles. "I noticed earlier today that these seem shorter than they should be." She set them on the table in the room, right in front of Elisabeth. "Do you call yourself a Christian?"

Elisabeth's lip trembled as she nodded.

"How can you say you're a Christian when you lie to me like this? You've been up reading at night!"

Elisabeth tried to hold her emotions inside, but she

could feel them bubbling up. At first she felt sadness and regret as Mammi kept yelling at her about her duties to her family. Then that sadness and regret changed into something else: anger. Elisabeth knew what would happen if her anger took control.

Mammi continued. "No Christian lies! How dare you think you can read at a time like this!"

Elisabeth could see Anna and Rosina huddled under the kitchen table, hugging each other. Luki had pulled the blanket over his head. All the children knew that when Mammi was angry, it was best to stay out of her way.

But Elisabeth wouldn't have it any more.

"I'm trying my best to balance everything! How come you have time to read the Bible on Sundays while Anna and I are at Margarethe-Néni's, tolerating that family's dislike of us? Jesus read, too, so why can't I?!"

Mammi's face turned crimson. "How dare you compare yourself to the Lord! He had a calling, to save us from our sins! He was to be a teacher of the people! Of course He read! Your calling is to be a wife and a mother! You do *not* need to read!"

She returned to the kitchen and Anna and Rosina huddled even closer together. Mammi opened a cupboard, pulled out a small, flat wooden box with a lid on it, slammed it on the floor, and opened the lid, exposing the dried corn kernels.

"For you!" she commanded Elisabeth.

Elisabeth stared at her siblings.

"Now!" Mammi commanded.

Elisabeth pushed down her knit stockings, lifted her skirt a little, and knelt in the corn.

CHAPTER NINE

"Wait," Juliana said to Dad. Staying in the car, she opened her dance bag and double-checked that she had her shoes. Twice.

"If you put this much effort into chores, you'd be done washing lettuce in ten minutes. Honestly, Juliana, that's the millionth time you've checked your bag today. You'll be fine."

"Can you just leave it with the lettuce? I can't make the same mistake twice. I'm not going to have any friends if I show up unprepared."

"But you'll always have family. That's it, isn't it?"

Juliana glowered at him. "Can we drop this? I told you yesterday what I think and I really don't want to start that up again." She checked her bag again.

Dad placed a hand on her shoulder. "You need some

perspective. You're stressing out over nothing, and before you tell me I don't get it, I do."

No, you don't, she thought. But as their argument yesterday replayed in her mind on fast forward, she remembered how little she knew about her dad. Maybe she should be the one to drop it. This time, at least.

Dad shooed her out of the car. "I've gotta grab some stuff still from the trucking company. They close in half an hour. Trust your father: you'll be fine."

Juliana turned her attention back to that front door. She didn't want to go in there; the car was much safer. Would anyone even speak to her?

"They're just shoes," Dad said. "Get going or you're coming with me, which means you'll miss practice, and I'm sure they would kick you out for that."

"It's more than just shoes!"

Dad rolled his eyes. "Think of it this way: being a good teammate also means that you have to give them a second chance."

Juliana hadn't thought of it that way. She nodded, actually thankful for the advice, zipped her bag shut, and got out of the car. Once she was at the studio door, she took a quick look back and watched Dad already turning the corner at the end of the street. She gulped and walked in.

So far, so good. Juliana had made it fully prepared to class. She'd even felt slightly confident when stretching: although everyone on the team already had their splits, and several could even bend their back leg so their foot met their head, Juliana was close: she only had a few centimetres left before she was flat on the ground, and on both sides to boot! It was just a matter of time and practice.

But barely anyone said anything to her. A few friendly glances and hellos here and there, but that was it. And to top it off, there were now twenty-four people in the class; a few hadn't made it yesterday because the storm had cut off the rural roads to their homes and those roads hadn't been cleared in time.

Miss Denise instructed everyone to stand in a circle and say their name again.

"I'm Riley."

"I'm Alex."

"Isaac."

"Janine."

"Jasmine."

Juliana stopped paying attention after Jasmine. Jasmine had a confidence about herself that Juliana found both intimidating and admirable. She was also clearly the best dancer on the team. Jasmine made eye contact with her and Juliana looked away abruptly. She'd been caught staring.

Strike two, she thought to herself.

"I'm Angel."

"Mackenzie."

"Ben."

There was a pause.

Juliana jumped. "Oh, sorry." She hadn't realized that the circle had come around to her. Her cheeks burned. "I'm Juliana."

The circle continued, and Juliana did her best to pay attention. At the end, Miss Denise nodded. "All right. Let's take it from the top, everyone."

The class rushed to their opening positions before Juliana could even take a step.

"Juliana, we're going to put you at the back. It'll be easier for you to learn." Miss Denise pointed to a spot upstage right. "Riley, Alex, shift down...exactly."

The back? Juliana knew many studios placed the weakest students at the back so they'd be less visible to the judges. Miss Kasia, on the contrary, believed everyone deserved a chance to shine. Had Juliana chosen a "bad to the back" studio?

"No debate," Miss Denise said. "It's just because you're new."

Juliana's face burned again. *Strike three*, she thought and stared at the floor as she headed to her new spot.

During the next two minutes, Miss Denise reviewed the first thirty-two counts with everyone and included a few pointers of what the others could do better. She turned on the music. Juliana's heart pounded: Miss Denise taught so fast that Juliana could barely remember the first steps. Staring into the mirror didn't help either: instead of twenty-four strangers, she now saw forty-eight.

Juliana kept her eyes glued to Miss Denise, who was nodding her head in time with the beat during the intro. Then she raised her hands and clapped the last four counts.

"Five, six, seven, eight!"

And within the next four counts, Juliana had to spring to the side to get out of everyone's way.

Miss Denise stopped the music.

"Jasmine, take Juliana into another studio and begin showing her up to here," and Miss Denise demonstrated a part in the dance with her hands, scatting a few syllables, to indicate to Jasmine where in the dance she meant. Jasmine nodded.

Juliana swallowed. *At least I've got the right shoes*, she thought hopelessly as she followed Jasmine out.

JULIANA SLAMMED HER FOOT INTO THE FLOOR. "I JUST CAN'T get this!"

She caught Jasmine rolling her eyes. "You know, you'd find this easier if you'd stop focusing on not getting it."

"Easy for you to say," Juliana said. "You're incredible."

"I've also had four months to learn it. You've had thirty minutes and a day without shoes so far. Now, do the pirouette."

Who did this girl think she was? God's gift to dance? *Well, actually*...Juliana had to admit that she was. She tendued out to second, did a ronde de jambe to fourth, and placed her foot. Then she stopped. If there was one thing she hated doing in tap shoes, it was pirouettes: she always lost control of her rotation.

"What?" Jasmine asked. "You're getting tripped up on tiny details that don't matter at this point."

"What do you mean they don't matter? If I don't get those tiny details, I'll bring the group down. Right now, I can't get my balance on the stupid pirouette."

"What did you do at your old studio?"

Juliana's chin dropped and she stared at the floor. "We only did doubles, and I could barely hang on there."

Jasmine crossed her arms and dug her gaze into Juliana, and Juliana wondered if this was what books meant when they described fear piercing your heart. "You'll bring the group down today if you don't learn this choreography. No one's going to care if you don't get your triple today, but they are going to care if you're in the wrong spot when they go into the turning riff sequence."

What were the other dancers like? Was Juliana going to have to defend herself like this to all of them?

"Listen," Jasmine said. "I'm not trying to be mean—I'm

just being realistic. You're not going to get better if you keep focusing on the wrong stuff. Let's skip the pirouette and move on. You know it comes here, and that's all you need to know today."

And she began to show Juliana the next thirty-two counts, her taps blurring in Juliana's eyes.

"My god, you're amazing," Juliana said. *She looks like she does this in her sleep*, she thought.

"Just takes practice," Jasmine said.

Yeah, probably in a home studio, five hours a day.

"I'll slow it down for you," Jasmine said.

She definitely thinks I'm stupid, Juliana thought.

LATER THAT DAY, JULIANA TOOK ADVANTAGE OF A FEW HOURS before supper to practice. She stared at the old shag carpet on the basement floor and the low ceiling. The space she had to practice was less than optimal.

But she had to make this work. She knew she had been trying Jasmine's patience, and after dancing with the rest of the group for another hour, Juliana had caught looks and side glances toward her. She had become *that* dancer in only two practices.

Dance for Juliana was like air. Some of her school friends back home loved sports, others their dogs, but for Juliana it was dance, the way the music washed over her body and flooded her pores, electrifying her with energy that filled her with life. Both the time she had broken her wrist and sprained her ankle in competition and then the recent cross-country ride from Alberta to Ontario with her parents proved to her that not dancing equalled prison. She liked most subjects at school, too, but learning didn't give her the feeling of disappearing into something greater than herself that dance did, a feeling she couldn't describe to anyone who didn't share it.

But at Kitchener Dance Academy, she had met twenty-four dancers who were greater than her. She had to reach their level and fast.

"Okay, let's get going," she said to herself. "Getting better doesn't happen on its own."

She stretched for ten minutes, aiming to reach just a little lower in her splits. Next followed several warm-up exercises for her feet in order to loosen up her ankles and activate her thighs and calves. She didn't have the music yet for this tap routine, but she had heard it enough today that she could hear it in her mind. Unfortunately, though, she only had her small tap board as her practice space. It made her attempts at her triple pirouette impossible because no matter how much she tried to convince herself that the tap board was not the edge of a stage, her body insisted that it was and that it risked falling into the non-existent audience if she lost her balance.

Which meant she lost her balance. Every time.

She wiped the sweat off her forehead and Jasmine's words echoed in her mind: "You're getting tripped up on the tiny details that don't matter at this point."

Juliana's shoulders stiffened. That dancer was getting on her case at the studio, and now she was invading Juliana's mind.

She tried the pirouette again and fell out of it.

"Fine," she said to herself. "I'll just start from the beginning."

Doing the first twenty seconds or so of the dance on the spot was hard, but Juliana began to feel the flow of the steps. And when it came to the pirouette, she just pulled up into retiré and didn't rotate.

"Juliana?"

Why did he have to interrupt her now? Juliana turned around, making sure she had a smile pasted on her face by the time she faced Opa. "I didn't hear you come in," she said.

Opa smiled back. "Your mom was right."

Juliana furrowed her brow.

"When you first arrived here," he said, "Katy said I would see you dance and that it would be wonderful. She's right."

Juliana blushed. His compliment was the last thing she'd expected but also the first good thing about her dancing she'd heard all day.

"Can you keep dancing?" he asked. "I want to see more. We didn't dance like this at home."

Now Juliana's smile turned into a real one: she couldn't be angry at him for that, and, to be honest, her practicing was becoming tense.

"It won't be my best," she said. She didn't want to raise his expectations.

"Why not?"

Juliana was worried about insulting Opa if she told him the truth, that his basement wasn't the best place for dance.

"I'm just tired, that's all," she said.

He studied her face for a moment and then wagged his finger at her. "Your Omama had a habit of saying too much. You don't say enough. Be honest with me, Yulika. You won't kill me."

Juliana felt awkward at having been caught lying to her grandfather, even if her intentions were good, but she remembered his embarrassment at how dirty his basement had been when they had first arrived. She wouldn't share the truth with him, not on this one thing, anyway.

"No, really, Opa, it's been a long day."

Opa sighed. "Omama's mouth sometimes got her into trouble. She even had to kneel in corn because of it. But she always spoke her mind. I think it's healthy."

Opa's comments caught Juliana's attention. "Kneel in corn?"

Opa laughed. "Back then, if you were bad, you kneeled in dry corn kernels. On your bare knees, of course."

Juliana's eyes popped open and Opa nodded. "It made sure you listened to your parents. Nowadays kids scream everywhere and run all over stores touching everything. But not back then." He laughed as his mind traveled back. "You know what? We never danced like what you do. We always danced in partners. And always to live music."

"It sounds like you had fun."

"We did, Yulika!" Suddenly his eyes opened wide in panic. "Music! How could I forget?"

And he shuffled upstairs as fast as his seventy-year-old legs could carry him.

Curious, Juliana followed Opa upstairs.

"What music?" she asked him.

"Radio," he replied curtly. He pulled the radio out of the living room and set it on the kitchen counter. He plugged it in and flicked the switch on.

The most horrendous music Juliana had ever heard came blaring out of its ancient speakers and she had to cover her ears. A mix of trumpet and accordion and Lord knows whatever other instruments played some kind of noisy tune. A march, maybe?

Upon seeing her reaction, Opa turned the volume down a little.

"I'm sorry," he said. "I still need to get used to you living here."

Juliana lowered her hands, but more out of politeness than desire. "What is that?"

Mom and Dad entered the kitchen.

"German hour?" Mom asked, grabbing a granola bar.

Opa nodded. "Only four hours every weekend now."

"Makes you want to dance, doesn't it?" Mom asked Juliana, and Juliana stared in amazement at the question. She wasn't being serious, was she?

"Yulika was dancing downstairs," Opa said. "I think she should dance for our family tonight! The way she moves her feet, I think it would fit the music!"

Opa looked so happy at his suggestion, Juliana wondered if his dentures would fall out. Thankfully, though, Dad saved her.

"She's not used to that kind of music," he said.

She flashed him a silent thank-you look, and Dad nodded.

A new song played.

"A polka!" Mom exclaimed cheerily. Mom grabbed Opa's hands, and the two automatically took up traditional ballroom positions. The tiny space of the kitchen forced them to just hop back and forth on their feet on the spot.

"Um, I think I should go back and practice," Juliana said, and she slipped back into the basement.

CHAPTER TEN

*I*f any good had come out of the past few days, it was that Elisabeth didn't have to help with wedding preparations: everyone understood that with Luki sick she was needed at home. However, that meant Rosina had to accompany Anna to their aunt and uncle's house to help. This worried Elisabeth: Anna was still too young to keep a good eye on her sister, who could get into trouble just for doing things that a six-year-old would do.

Elisabeth paused for a moment and looked out the kitchen window into her neighbour's yard and then ladled some soup into a bowl. One thing Elisabeth missed was a connection to the bigger world. Without Tata here, men from the other families didn't come by in the evening to play *skat* and to debate topics that didn't involve dresses, shoes, or noses. Moreover, she couldn't even leave Luki to go hear the postman when he arrived on his weekly visit to deliver mail and shout out any headlines people wanted to hear. She was caged in.

"But I don't mean it that way!" she whispered to Jesus over the door. Of course she was thankful that Luki had improved somewhat, and she rejoiced for her cousin's wedding. But when did Elisabeth get to matter? When was it her turn to do what she wanted?

She brought the bowl of soup to Luki, who was sitting up in his bed. His cheekbones stuck out after several days of eating nothing. But then this afternoon, after another long sleep, he had asked for something to eat, which almost made Elisabeth cry: it was the first sign that Jesus was indeed watching over them.

"I've been praying for you every day," she told him as she fed him.

Luki swallowed the spoonful and smiled.

"Mammi's been busy making shoes for wedding guests," Elisabeth said. "She's earning money for us."

Luki nodded as he swallowed the next spoonful. "Tata?" he asked. His voice was still weak.

Elisabeth shrugged her shoulders. "I'm sorry, Luki, I don't know. We haven't heard anything at all."

Luki's eyes looked sad.

"But," Elisabeth said, "maybe he's earning so much money that he hasn't had time to write us yet." She fed him another spoonful.

Luki's eyes lit up. "Do you think so?"

Elisabeth shrugged again. "Why must we always think of the worst? Jesus cured lepers, helped blind men see, and no matter how people treated Him, He always talked about God and Heaven and all the good things that are up there. And He has answered our prayers, because you're doing better! Maybe we should think a little more like Him."

Deep coughs overtook Luki's body, and Elisabeth handed him a handkerchief so he could spit anything out that came up.

"Keep praying for Tata," she said, "but also rest."

He coughed. "And you'll pray for me?"

Elisabeth smiled and nodded. As she finished feeding him the soup, she prayed silently: *Jesus, please continue to watch over us.*

ELISABETH TOOK A MOMENT TO REST IN THE KITCHEN. SHE would not nap, but at least she could rest. Mammi was out in the workshop, and after the other day, Elisabeth dared not again fall asleep until bedtime. She had also stopped staying up late at night, which made it easier for her to stay awake during the day.

The house was eerily quiet, as though everyone had died. The only proof that everyone was still alive was the lack of a coffin in the back room. Her eyes shifted between the crucifix over the door to the front room and Luki on his bed in there.

So far as Elisabeth knew, Mammi had had several children who had died, including Anna's twin sister, Rosina. And because Anna's twin had died shortly after birth, Mammi's next daughter was named Rosina to make sure Mammi's great aunt, Rosina-Néni, was still honoured in their family. Would God allow Mammi to have another child if Luki died from this illness? And would it be a boy so that Tata's name would continue in the family?

Elisabeth slapped herself in the face. "I just told Luki to stop having such thoughts. I should do the same."

She took a drink of water to freshen up and then got to work. First, she would make a strong chamomile tea for Luki when he woke up. She slipped on her boots and brought in water from the well outside. Once back in the house, she put her house shoes on, set the kettle on the stove, and poured water into it and then set the lid on.

"And next?" she said to herself.

Luki's pants and shirts on the table caught her eye, and she removed some hot coals from the oven, put them into the iron, and then placed the iron on the stove while it heated up.

"That's heating up...now what?"

Her voice travelled through their three-room house without receiving an answer. She couldn't start preparing supper until the ironing was done: she needed the kitchen table for both activities, and Mammi would certainly make her kneel in the corn again if Elisabeth got the wash dirty. But would she finish the ironing in time to begin cooking supper? She chose to push the washing bowl to the side so she could use that table to chop vegetables.

The lid on the pot of water began to jiggle, so Elisabeth removed the pot from the burner, pulled down a small canister of dried chamomile flowers from a shelf over the oven, tossed a few tablespoons into the water, and replaced the lid. She then waved her hand underneath it to test the heat.

"Almost," she said, placing it back the stove. In the meantime, she spread out Luki's pants and folded the pant legs so the pleats would be nice and smooth.

"I wonder who's ironing Tata's pants?" she said to Jesus on the crucifix above the door. "Does he have help with that? Or does he have to pay someone to do it? Or maybe he repairs their shoes and they iron his clothes?"

Jesus looked painfully, silently down at her.

As Elisabeth grabbed the iron from the stove, she glanced out the window and almost jumped for joy: Maria, her best friend in all of Semlak was walking up the side of the house. Maria was a year older than Elisabeth and herself had only one brother. Friends since Elisabeth could remember, it felt like Elisabeth had become Maria's only sister and Maria, Elisabeth's older sister.

Elisabeth swung the door open and was ready to throw

herself into Maria's arms. Then she stopped herself: Maria was carrying a large pot in both her hands.

"Careful!" Maria said, her smile as big as Elisabeth's, placing the pot on the stove. "My brother came home from school sick last week. Mammi had heard through Meier Josef that Luki was ill, so we made a big pot of soup and wanted to share some of it with you. We know it's especially hard without your Tata around."

Elisabeth was ready to cry. She wouldn't have to cook so much for supper!

"Oh, thank you, Maria!" she said, giving her best friend a tight hug. Elisabeth wiped her hands on her apron before taking Maria's winter shawl and mittens to the back room. "How is your brother doing now?"

"He's eating again," she said, although her face turned sad despite the good news. "But our neighbour's baby may not make it."

Elisabeth could already hear church bells in her head.

Maria clapped her hands. "Now, how can I help you?"

Elisabeth took a moment to survey the kitchen and decide what needed to be done next: the tea was cooking, she was already ironing...

"Could you start some bread?"

"Get me an apron!"

Elisabeth retrieved an apron from a drawer in the front room. "By the way, do you have any tips for making a rum roll?"

Maria smiled. "Actually, I do."

Three hours later, Elisabeth had ironed Luki's and Mammi's clothing, had taken soup and some of yesterday's bread out to Mammi in the workshop, and had given Luki some tea before he fell asleep again. Maria popped two loaves of risen white bread into the oven.

Maybe Elisabeth would finally have some time to read.

CHAPTER ELEVEN

*N*ew Year's Eve, and Mom's family had arrived to celebrate: Uncle Peter, and Aunt Anne and Uncle Phillip with all six kids. Opa had been talking about their celebration all day, including begging Juliana to dance for his family. But now that she knew how weak her dancing was, she refused.

Juliana wore a cream dress that reached mid-thigh and she had put on light make-up. She'd even taken the time to straighten her hair. But in part still embarrassed by the events of Christmas Eve, and in part scared Opa was going to make her dance in front of everyone, Juliana couldn't face her family and instead sat in her room, texting with Rachel.

So practice was better today?

Yeah but still lots to learn

They're that good?

Amazing! Backs like elastics

Wow!

Not sure I can catch up

Of course u can!

U rock but you haven't seen them especially Jasmine

When her phone didn't show blinking dots that let her know Rachel was typing, Juliana scrolled through the conversation to see if she'd said anything wrong. She couldn't find anything, but then the three dots appeared at the bottom. She watched them flicker as Rachel typed from the other side of the country.

Your new friend?

Juliana panicked. Jasmine wasn't her new friend! Jasmine probably didn't even like her! The last thing she'd wanted was to make Rachel worry about their friendship, which reached back years to when they'd first started dance.

Noooo! You're my friend. She's just a crazy awesome dancer. NOT my friend

Rachel sent a smiley emoji through and then continued typing. *I'd be really sad if she was*

No one can replace you Rach!

And she meant it. Juliana and Rachel had been through thick and thin together, from Rachel's parents' divorce to tough judges at dance competitions to Juliana's move out east.

Go they're waiting

I can't

You're finally discovering your family go

The door to Juliana's room reminded her of a drawbridge from some old cartoon that creaked as it opened slowly, and you knew that some dangerous monster was behind it. But instead of monsters the Roths, Morgans, and Schuhmachers waited for her. And Sophie, too, of course.

I hardly know them, she typed to Rachel.

A knock on the door.

It was Dad. "Look, Juliana, we've allowed you to sit in here by yourself for at least half an hour. It's time you joined us."

Juliana's phone vibrated with Rachel's next text. Juliana glanced at it.

I'm always here for u!

Juliana sent her a thumbs-up and a wave goodbye. She threw her phone on to her bed but not before reading Rachel's last message one more time. The text left Juliana wondering if Rachel could truly be there for her.

Always.

JULIANA WALKED DOWN THE SHORT HALLWAY TO THE KITCHEN.

"Well, howdy stranger!" Uncle Peter said in a not-so-funny cowboy accent. He flashed a big smile that made Juliana wonder if his lips might ever snap from being stretched so much.

But she smiled in return. "Hi, Uncle Peter."

Aunt Anne opened her arms wide and gave Juliana a hug. Afterwards, Juliana worked her way from the kitchen to the living room, where she greeted all her cousins and Uncle Phillip. The only place left for her to sit was next to Sophie. But Juliana didn't just want to drop down onto the couch and scare her. Could Sophie see that Juliana was standing in front of her? Was Juliana supposed to say she was going to sit down? Juliana had a hard time understanding just how much Sophie could and couldn't see. To her, blind had meant seeing nothing at all; she had never thought that blind could mean seeing some things and not others.

"Hi, Juliana," Sophie said. "Did you do anymore shovelling today?"

Juliana smiled and shook her head. After a moment, she realized Sophie hadn't reacted and spoke her answer instead. "Sorry, um, no, nothing today. Dad did it." Now that Juliana knew that Sophie had seen her, she sat down.

A moment of silence passed between the two of them.

"Um, did you shovel anymore at home?"

Sophie shook her head. "Dean looked after it today, and Scott helped."

"Cool."

The two cousins sat in silence for a few minutes while everyone else around them talked.

"Juliana," Mom called from the kitchen, "I need your help: I've got to look after the goulash here."

"Sorry, uh, I have to go," Juliana said, kind of happy to leave the awkwardness of the moment but also a little disappointed: a quick glance around the room told Juliana that everyone else was engrossed in conversation and Juliana had barely said a word to Sophie. Now that she thought of it, when she'd first entered the tiny living room, nobody had been talking to Sophie then either.

"So I heard. Do you want any help?"

Juliana froze. On the one hand, having someone close to her age to talk to would be nice. On the other hand, the tiny kitchen was an absolute chaotic mess. How would Sophie navigate it without hurting herself? And what was she going to do? Chop carrots and slice off her finger?

"Juliana?" Sophie asked.

"Uh..."

Sophie stood up and faced Juliana, her eyes focused on her, which surprised Juliana, because it made Sophie not look blind. "I'm not disabled," she whispered. "I can help."

Juliana's shoulders pulled up and she suddenly wished she were a turtle. Or perhaps a gopher. Just an animal that could somehow hide. Even an ostrich would do, so she wouldn't have to see the others in the room, who were now staring at her again, just like on Christmas Eve.

But Juliana wasn't going to run like she had last week. She had to say something, but it had to be something that wouldn't land her kneeling in a pile of corn kernels either. Metaphorically speaking, anyway. She just didn't want Sophie to hurt herself. She was only twelve and if she couldn't see in front of her, then how could she help in the kitchen? If there was one thing Mom always reminded Juliana about, it was to keep her eyes on the knife.

But she couldn't say those kinds of things, and Sophie seemed independent anyway. Dad had taken that moment yesterday to share a tiny piece of himself with her. Maybe she could try that with Sophie.

"I'm sorry. It's been a tough week for me. I was just worried that, um, you know, you might hurt yourself."

Although Sophie didn't exactly smile, her expression relaxed. "I may not be a celebrity chef, but I can chop a carrot or two."

"Okay, sure. I could use your help."

Sophie smiled, and now Juliana relaxed. "The kitchen's a bit of a mess, though," she warned, "so just be a bit careful."

"Thanks," Sophie said, without any hint of sarcasm or displeasure.

"You can cut the carrots," Mom said to Juliana when

they got to the kitchen. "Sophie, could you wash the lettuce?"

Sophie smiled. "That's my favourite job!"

Juliana had to smile in spite of herself and felt instantly happier about Sophie being there.

"Thanks for your help, girls. I haven't made goulash in probably twenty years and I want to get it right. I even hunted down Hungarian paprika at a European foods store."

Mom went back to stand at the stove, dropping bits of beef into a reddish soup Juliana had never seen before. It smelled good. Was this something Mom would have grown up with? Or maybe even Opa? Juliana watched her mom out of the corner of her eye—while still paying attention to her knife—to see what ingredients she used.

"Listen," Juliana said to Sophie. "I should tell you something."

"That you've got a third leg?"

"Uh..."

Sophie stared ahead while she worked, her fingers helping her find the mushy parts on the leaves of lettuce. "It was a joke," she said.

Juliana grinned and then remembered she needed to say what she was feeling. "That's funny. But no, that's not it."

"You've never really met a blind person before?"

"Yeah, I haven't. So, I don't really know how to help or

when not to help or...well, all that awkward stuff. There's just a lot I don't know, and I don't like feeling that way."

"Well, ask away!" Sophie said jubilantly. "I'm all ears!"

Juliana didn't have to say what she was feeling. She groaned at the bad joke and then both girls giggled.

CHAPTER TWELVE

A week had passed, and Luki was finally eating full bowls of chicken soup, slices of bread—but only with paprika, no butter—and even little bits of pork. His tiny frame saddened Elisabeth: his collar bones and cheekbones protruded like broom handles and his hair was matted to his head after not having been washed in such a long time.

He crept into the kitchen and paused in the doorway to rest. "Can I have more bread?" he asked, his voice weak.

Elisabeth stopped kneading the bread dough she had been working on and sliced a piece from the morning's loaf.

"Go back to your bed," she instructed him. "I'll bring it to you."

Luki turned around and dragged his bony little body back to bed.

"You are looking down on us," she said to Jesus and sprinkled a little paprika on Luki's slice of bread.

Mammi came in from Tata's workshop out back. "How is he doing?" she asked, wiping her hands on her apron.

"He just asked for more to eat," Elisabeth answered.

Mammi's face relaxed and her hands dropped to her side. "You looked after him well. He'll make it now, that much is for sure. I think you can help with the wedding again." She nodded in approval and then returned to the workshop.

Elisabeth smiled.

It was Saturday, and Elisabeth and Anna were again at their aunt and uncle's home. "You make sure those cookies are perfect, Elisabeth," Konrad-Bátschi commanded.

"Of course," she replied, keeping her eyes focused on her work: baking sweet *mandelkipfel*, from almond meal and flour. Konrad-Bátschi stood as tall as Tata, but because of his trade, had a body twice the size of her father's.

"Every *kipfel* shaped perfectly and the same size."

Again, Elisabeth nodded. She rolled a small amount of almond dough in her hands, making sure the middle stayed fat and the ends thin, lay it on the baking sheet, and formed it into a small crescent.

Margarethe-Néni came out of the back room and immediately got to work alongside Elisabeth, Anna, and Susi. Gretche was at the stove, stirring a broth and chopping vegetables for soup. Georg and Samuel followed her, dressed in their winter coats.

"Margarethe, we're heading over to Meier Josef for a schnapps," Konrad-Bátschi said, and as much as Elisabeth didn't like her uncle, she wished she could join him: no reading, no drawing, and only one visit from a friend throughout Luki's illness had left Elisabeth feeling like she was drowning in a sea of gossip. But when Konrad-Bátschi and his two sons left the house, Elisabeth's chest relaxed and Anna let out an audible sigh.

Does he have any idea how hard it is to make these all so exact? she thought to herself. The answer was obvious: he didn't know, because he'd never made *mandelkipfel* in his life and never would.

"You heard your uncle," Margarethe-Néni said.

Several minutes of silence followed as everyone rolled dough. Once the cookies were baked, they would be wrapped up in cloths and taken to the cold cellar behind the house. The wedding was this coming Tuesday, only a few days away now, and Elisabeth had to somehow juggle Luki's improving health, continue helping with wedding preparations, and run her household.

"Elisabeth," Susi said, "would you mind getting me some cloths? They're in the back room, in the dresser on the top right drawer. Mine are getting too greasy."

Elisabeth dusted off her hands on her apron and headed into the back room. Her aunt and uncle's house didn't differ much from Elisabeth's except that they had more crocheted doilies, knitted blankets, and embroidered pillowcases. But with all three daughters all grown up, that was hardly a surprise.

She opened the drawer and pulled out a few tea towels. When she lifted the last one, she stopped. Underneath it was an envelope addressed to Konrad-Bátschi.

It was from Tata.

Elisabeth's heart stopped. *So he had survived the journey! Thank you, Jesus!*

She checked the postage date on it and gasped: he had written the letter four weeks ago! But did this letter mean Mammi had also heard from Tata? Then why hadn't she said anything? Could she have forgotten?

No, of course not! Elisabeth thought to herself. How could she forget something like this? And as mean as Mammi could be, surely she wouldn't hide something like this from the children? Unless Tata's letter to her contained terrible news. If only she could read the letter...

"Did you find them?" Susi called back.

Elisabeth took a deep breath to calm herself and slid the drawer closed. Each step into the kitchen felt like she was walking through thick mud that tried to hold her in place. Elisabeth couldn't believe that her aunt and uncle were so mean that they wouldn't tell her family about Tata's letter.

"Sorry," she said, her voice deceptively calm, as she came into the room with the cloths. "It took me a moment."

"But my daughter's instructions were clear," Margarethe-Néni said.

Elisabeth could only shrug her shoulders. "I'm sorry."

Susi placed the cloths on the cooking table next to their oven and Elisabeth returned to her baking duties.

Could she ask about the letter? Of course not. She'd have to admit she'd been snooping. But Tata was her father and she the eldest child, now in charge of the household. If something was wrong, shouldn't she find out about it so she could help her family?

"Remember," Margarethe-Néni said, "every *kipfel* must be perfect."

Elisabeth saw an opportunity and decided to milk it. "I will try but I'm distracted. We still haven't heard from Tata. It's been two months now."

Would Margarethe-Néni admit to the letter?

"I'm certain he's fine," she said.

Elisabeth saw another opportunity. She feigned a surprised look. "You've heard from him, then?"

Her aunt responded with an angry look. "Of course not. Obviously I would tell you if I had."

"I'm sorry," Elisabeth replied, remaining as innocent as she could. "I meant no insult." She returned to her baking.

Why was her aunt like this? Konrad-Bátschi had inherited the blacksmith shop from Otata, Elisabeth's grandfather. At every wedding Elisabeth had ever helped out with, Margarethe-Néni had peppered her brother- and sister-in-law with snide remarks and underhanded insults. Elisabeth was certain she even shared personal stories with Meier Josef, who could spread a rumour he'd heard before church so quickly that Elisabeth would hear it on the way home from service.

Suddenly, Gretche cried out as the pot of soup crashed onto the dirt-and-chaff floor and the broth spilled out everywhere. Elisabeth immediately rushed into the back room and grabbed more cloths out of the drawer.

"Here!" she said, waving them. If that broth soaked in, the floor would smell like chicken for weeks.

Gretche grabbed the cloths on the cooking table next to the stove and everyone helped dab up the mess immediately.

"You stupid cow!" Margarethe-Néni yelled at her grown daughter.

"I didn't do it on purpose!" Gretche replied. "The Devil took my arm and pushed the pot!"

"Then pray for Jesus' protection."

Gretche stood up and headed for the front room.

"After we finish cleaning up! Or did the Devil take your mind, too, like he's taken Georg's?" Margarethe-Néni said.

"I am not like my brother!" Gretche shouted. She scrubbed the floor with her dirty towels, retrieved a cloth sack from the front room and collected all the tea towels in it. She then stormed back into the front room, dropped onto her knees next to her bed, and began to pray. But Elisabeth stood close to the door and was certain she could hear her cousin instead asking God to punish Margarethe-Néni.

Margarethe-Néni and Susi returned to the kitchen table to keep baking, not even thanking Elisabeth and Anna for helping clean up the mess. It was as though dropping a pot was so embarrassing that they wanted to pretend like it had never happened.

"Anna," Elisabeth said, "why don't you start chopping vegetables for a fresh soup?"

Anna nodded, appearing grateful that her sister had given her a task. The basket of root vegetables was under the table and hadn't been touched by the spilled broth.

The first sheet of *mandelkipfel* was ready and Susi slid it in the oven. Elisabeth noticed they needed fresh tea towels in the kitchen now to pull things out of the oven, so she offered to get some.

Tata's letter and its envelope were on the floor: they must have fallen out when Elisabeth had ripped the pile of towels out of the drawer. She bent down to pick up both, then glanced back at her family, all of whom had their backs to her, and then up at Jesus, who was looking down at her.

The letter was none of her business; she knew that. But Tata had been gone for so long, and she so desired to hear from him...

She peeked into the kitchen again. Everyone was too engrossed in their feelings and their work to notice that Elisabeth hadn't returned yet.

She opened it.

Dear Konrad,

I arrived safe and am staying with one of Meier Josef's cousins. Please don't tell Lissa that I've written. If she or my family are scared because I haven't written, comfort them. You and I don't always agree on things, but we agree on how important family is. I trust you will do as I ask.

I haven't found a good job yet and I don't want Lissa to know. They don't like to hire people here who don't speak English. I've repaired a few shoes so far, but that's all. I wish to have happier news for her when I send her my first letter.

I hope all is well. Please write me and tell me how my family is doing, especially Elisabeth: I need to know that she's growing up and will soon be ready for a husband.

Your brother,

Lukas

THAT NIGHT, ELISABETH COULDN'T SLEEP. SHE HAD MANAGED to keep the letter's existence a secret for the day, but it was gnawing at her conscience: was the Fourth Commandment not "Honour your father and your mother"? But which parent should she honour in this situation? Her father's wish to not say anything to his wife? Or her mother's wish to hear news of her husband?

She lit a few candles in the back room and pulled down a book of Luther's teachings. Hopefully she would find an answer in there.

"Elisabeth!"

Elisabeth jumped, almost knocking over a candle. Mammi stood in the doorway, her own candle in hand, dressed in her nightgown, her long braid flowing down her back. The shadows from the flame deepened her wrinkles and creases, making her look angrier than usual.

"I told you not to read at night!" she whispered through gritted teeth.

Elisabeth didn't know what to say. Jesus required His followers to be honest at all times, and God required that children honour their parents. But she still had not answered her original question: which parent should she honour?

"Elisabeth, you can kneel in that corn for an hour or you can tell me what you're doing."

Elisabeth saw no way out. *Help me find the words*, she prayed. "Can we please sit down?" she asked. To her surprise, Mammi pulled out a chair.

Under the table, Elisabeth wiped her hands on her nightgown. "I saw something today and...I don't know what to do about it. I was hoping to find an answer in Martin Luther's teachings."

The crease between Mammi's eyebrows grew deeper. "Just what are you talking about?"

Elisabeth rubbed her hands together.

"I saw a letter from Tata at Konrad-Bátschi's." Elisabeth paused to let Mammi speak.

"What did it say?"

"This is why I'm confused, Mammi. God commands that we honour our parents, but your wishes and Tata's wishes are different, and I don't know what to do."

Mammi nodded. "I see. Then let me make it simple for you, Elisabeth. I am here right now, and I ask you to tell me what it said."

Elisabeth glanced up at Jesus and light flickering from their candles made it look like he was nodding to her. She decided to do as Mammi asked.

"The letter was mailed four weeks ago—I don't know when they received it. He said he hadn't found a job yet, that he didn't want to write you until he had good news, and..." Elisabeth could barely bring the last part over her lips. "He didn't want Konrad-Bátschi to tell you so you wouldn't worry even more."

The silence that followed frightened Elisabeth: Mammi always knew what to say. Even if it was something Elisabeth didn't want to hear—like a punishment if she didn't obey her mother—Mammi knew what to say.

This time, Mammi didn't. This time, Mammi sat before Elisabeth frozen, uncertain, scared.

But this time, Elisabeth knew what to do: she held Mammi's hand.

CHAPTER THIRTEEN

It was several days after New Year's Day, and Juliana was back at the studio. Jasmine sat on the floor in a 180-degree splat.

"What are your New Year's resolutions?" she asked.

The question surprised Juliana, who sat in pigeon pose, with one leg folded in front and the other extended behind her. She had New Year's resolutions, but they were written down in a special notebook, her book of goals for the year. She knew what she had written, though:

✓ *Get my splits*
✓ *Bend my back in half*
✓ *Make and keep 5 new friends in January*
✓ *Maintain 90% average at new school*
✓ *Raise competition average from 85% to 95%*

But she didn't want to share her goals with Jasmine,

whose resolutions were probably something like getting 100% in everything she did or winning several $5,000 scholarships at competition. But whatever Jasmine's goals were, Juliana preferred to keep hers secret; she didn't want anyone to know if she failed or gave up on them.

"I don't tell them to anyone," she said.

"Okay, everyone, up and to your positions!" Miss Denise said with a clap.

"If you don't share them, no one can help you achieve them," Jasmine replied.

The thought caught Juliana off guard and she barely heard Miss Denise count the dancers in. But once the music started, Juliana's mind snapped to one immediate goal: not screwing up. This was the third team practice she'd attended and she hadn't yet gotten the choreography perfect. She knew what happened to the weakest dancers on any team: they were ignored, even shunned, as though the team was some religious group. It didn't matter if you did your best; it only mattered if your skill matched everyone else's. Although Juliana believed she was already that dancer, she kept Dad's advice in her heart: to give her team a second chance, too. That meant, at least for today, emptying her mind of her worries.

She began the routine and kept up. When the chaîné-turn sequence came, though, her heart raced: a chassé followed by three turns, four times, and she had to make it through two lines of dancers and not hit a single one.

"Ow!" a boy yelled.

Juliana pulled her arms in and hit the brakes on her sequence. "Oh my god, I'm so sorry!"

"Juliana, keep going!" Miss Denise commanded, but Juliana had already lost track of where she was. Miss Denise stopped the music.

"Isaac, are you all right?" Miss Denise asked.

Isaac nodded, rubbing his shoulder.

"Sorry," Juliana said in a tiny voice.

"No problem," Isaac said, moving back to his opening position. Others followed, and Juliana followed them. Miss Denise didn't say a word, and Juliana was embarrassed that she had caused the restart.

"From the top," Miss Denise said and hit play.

This time, Juliana made it through the chaîné-turn sequence.

Then she fell out of her triple pirouette.

But this time, she kept going, and once she hit a section she hadn't been shown yet, she deftly jumped out of the way and stood at the side, taking note of the next few steps. When the group finished, Miss Denise said, "And again!" and they all obeyed. Juliana succeeded this time, with only minor mistakes, and even completed the following sixteen counts before she had to step out.

When the group finished, the studio fell quiet, except for the sound of everyone catching their breath.

By the end of the first hour, Juliana had added another thirty-two counts to what she already knew. She still had half the dance to go, but she could feel the choreography finally gelling. Sitting in the change room with the other girls, she was eating an apple and some pumpkin seeds when Jasmine sat next to her and patted Juliana on the back.

"I have to admit," she said, "I didn't think you'd be able to keep up."

Juliana froze, her mouth half open and a handful of seeds on its way to her lips. Why on earth would someone say something like that?

Miss Denise knocked on the door and called everyone back to class. The other girls shoved their snacks back into their bags, grabbed their water bottles, and rushed out before Juliana knew what was happening. However, Jasmine stayed behind to wait as Juliana packed her food away.

"When you showed up without your shoes, I honestly thought you were some lazy dancer."

Juliana didn't know if she should cry out in jubilation because she had been right about what Jasmine thought or to pack her bags and head home whimpering. Apparently, something showed on her face, though, because Jasmine put her hand on Juliana's shoulder. Her voice was gentle.

"I'm sorry. I really don't mean to insult you. I just don't waste time beating around the bush. You really surprised me today, and I think it's awesome. It's the holidays, when all our friends at school are hanging out at home, texting with friends, playing video games, doing all that fun stuff, and we're here. You're here. You just started here several days ago, and you've already got half the dance down."

Juliana calmed down. Jasmine's intent seemed sincere. But what should she say in response? If it was the wrong thing, she'd be on the shunning list again.

They walked down the hall to the studio.

Opening up to Sophie had helped, so maybe trying it here wasn't a bad idea, either. After all, Juliana didn't have to tell Jasmine her life story, just something small that was important to her.

"I just arrived about two weeks ago from Calgary, so I haven't had as much time to practice as I'd like: unpacking, meeting new family, all that stuff."

Jasmine looked surprised. "Really?"

"We arrived three days before Christmas."

"Miss Denise said you had recently moved here, but I had no idea you had *just* moved here. And you came all the way across the country?"

Juliana smiled and nodded. "And we've moved in with my grandfather. The house is smaller and a lot older than ours back home. I don't even have a room to really practice in now."

They entered the studio.

"That's a lot. Then I take it all back: you're doing *a lot* better than I would expect under those circumstances."

Miss Denise clapped her hands again. "Enough chit-chat. But yes, Juliana, you're doing very well."

Juliana smiled at her new teacher. Miss Denise continued. "Successful dancers don't make it just because of great technique but because of tenacity. If you keep this up, you may have what it takes to make a career of this."

Juliana beamed. "Really?"

Miss Denise nodded.

"Jasmine, take her into the next studio and show her the next section."

BACK AT HOME, JULIANA STOOD IN FRONT OF HER CLOSET mirror. Freshly washed, her brown hair hung in long clumps over her shoulders and down her back. She had on a fresh pair of denim leggings, a t-shirt that said, "I dance because I exist," and a fair-trade beaded necklace Rachel had given her.

She had never given much thought to a professional career in dance: no one had ever told her it was possible, but now that Miss Denise had said it...

"What do I want?" she asked herself in the mirror. "What do I really, really want?"

She reached for her book of goals and reviewed her list. If she was going to make dance a career, she'd have to do more than just get her splits and high marks at competition. But she was also a good student. For the most part, she enjoyed school, though tests and exams perhaps not so much. But then, who did? She had thought in the past about being a doctor, maybe a physiotherapist. Maybe she would spend a summer on exchange in Australia or go to a French camp in Quebec before she decided everything.

Working as a doctor or physiotherapist would be a career for life. If she danced professionally, she'd have to start a new career by her late thirties. And her body would likely be very broken. She remembered once taking a master class from a former prima ballerina whose legs were permanently frozen in turnout, and Juliana had read about other retired dancers who had arthritis in their feet, had to have their hips replaced—or both! What good was dancing professionally if you had to stop at some point and deal with a permanently injured body for the rest of your life?

Juliana set her book of goals down and opened her great-grandmother's book of drawings to the sketch of the wedding. Opa had said the other day that every girl aspired to marry and become a wife and then a mother.

She looked at herself in the mirror again, twirled her hair into a makeshift bun, holding it up with one hand, and tried to picture herself with a bonnet on. Then she let her hair drop.

"I don't know what I want when I grow up, but it's definitely not that."

Juliana closed the book and placed it back in the drawer in her nightstand. She dropped on to her bed and began texting Rachel. She didn't want to tell her about how fantastic practice had gone today. She didn't want Rachel to worry about their friendship again—the two of them were BFFs. But Miss Kasia had never told Juliana that she could ever turn professional. She decided to just text her friend a question.

What do you actually want to be when you grow up?

Knowing it was roughly lunchtime back in Calgary, Juliana didn't expect an answer immediately, so she called up one of her social media accounts and posted the same question to her friends.

Then, exhausted from the day's practice, she nodded off.

JULIANA RUBBED HER EYES, STRETCHED OUT, AND ROLLED over to see Mom standing over her.

"Tired, eh, sweetie?"

Juliana nodded.

"Sorry to wake you, but the snow's really coming down,

and I need your help. You can shovel or help in the kitchen. What would you prefer?"

Juliana groaned and stretched. "Shovel," she said.

Mom smiled. "I figured as much. Take your time, but not too much time, okay?"

Juliana nodded, and Mom left the room.

Remembering what she'd texted and posted, she swiped open her phone. Rachel had responded.

Why?

Juliana typed back.

Sorry. Was sleeping. Just curious. Not important.

She then opened her social media account and her eyes popped open.

Start-up CEO

Mechanic

Don't know. Hate school.

Who cares? Live in the now! #carpediem

Astronaut #nasa

Garbage collector—always wanted to ride on the side of those trucks

Travel to #Africa first

ur an idiot dumb question the future is dead

POTUS

Help poor kids

A woman

PM, not POTUS

Freedom fighter for kids

The list went on and on, with answers from more than just her friends. Although marked by a few trolls and some smart remarks, the list was as diverse in ideas as her old school was in students.

"Juliana!" Mom called.

"Coming!" She slipped on some warmer socks and stopped for another moment in front of the mirror.

"How am I ever going to decide what to do with my life?"

CHAPTER FOURTEEN

Elisabeth stood in front of the looking glass in the front room of Konrad-Bátschi and Margarethe-Néni's house and brushed back a few wisps of her hair. She had on her white dress, which had a lightly ruffled collar, long sleeves, and, as all dresses did, a pressed apron, also white. The front half of her blonde hair was pulled back into two braids that joined the rest of her hair in one long braid that folded over itself and was pinned to the top of her head. To make her hair look more festive than usual, Elisabeth had added a white-beaded hairband.

Outside, she could hear the small marching band coming down the street for the bride and everyone else in the house. She peeked out the window and saw a sizeable crowd of perhaps thirty or so men and a handful of women laughing and joyfully walking along through the snow and slush down the street.

She turned to Susi. No matter what Elisabeth thought of her relatives, a wedding was always cause for celebration, and today was no different. Another girl was about to become a woman.

"So?" she said, her voice full of excitement. "Are you ready?"

The other women and girls in the room—Eva, Gretche, Anna, Rosina, Margarethe-Néni, Mammi, and several young cousins from Margarethe-Néni's side—all stared at Susi, who nodded so much that the white floral wreath on her head almost fell off.

"Careful!" Elisabeth said and helped Susi put it back in place.

Konrad-Bátschi was in the back room, waiting with an open bottle of the wedding wine to share with the crowd of male guests who would arrive any moment.

Mammi tried to smile for her niece, but Elisabeth could tell that her mother was boiling inside: no one had even said a word of comfort as Tata had asked them to in his letter. Elisabeth also believed that Mammi somehow felt betrayed, that after sixteen years of marriage, Tata didn't trust her to handle such sad news. Elisabeth knew Tata had acted with good intent, but how could he not know his wife after so long?

Although Mammi's mood did not become apparent to

the wedding guests, Elisabeth had seen it for days. It had begun the morning after Elisabeth had confessed everything. Mammi was dressed and busying about before any of the children had awoken, and when Elisabeth looked at the clock, she saw Mammi had let them all sleep in. Over the following days, Mammi barely punished: when Rosina dropped a bowl of flour on the floor, all she had to do was clean it up. Mammi neither hit her nor demanded she kneel in the box of corn. Even when Anna forgot to feed the farm animals outside, all Mammi said was that she shouldn't forget her duties. She then gave Anna a light tap on the bum and sent her to feed the animals right away. Mammi moved through her days as though in a haze, barely noticing what was happening around her.

The music grew louder, and even usually quiet Anna and little Rosina became giddy. Margarethe-Néni smiled but otherwise remained still, as all older women did. Elisabeth wondered what went through her mind. Susi was her last child to marry off. Was her aunt happy? Sad? The marriage made her, in a way, no longer a mother.

The marching music blared through the front windows now and there was a bang on the door. Margarethe-Néni hurried over and opened it.

"We've come for the bride!" a young man announced as the music wound down. Margarethe-Néni stepped back and welcomed the whole party in.

The parade crowded into the house, spilling into all

three rooms. Rosina and Anna each picked up platters with pieces of cake and the *mandelkipfel* Elisabeth had helped bake and began passing them around to all the guests while Konrad-Bátschi passed out small servings of his homemade wine to the men. Luki, all healthy again, had arrived with the parade, too, having stayed with men from Mammi's side of the family. He looked up at Konrad-Bátschi, his eyes wide with desire, but Konrad-Bátschi shook his head.

"You're too young, yet. First, you need to become a good *skat* player!" He let out a hearty laugh, clapped Luki on the back, and continued serving the other men. Luki's face dropped in disappointment, but once Anna came around with a platter of sweet goods, it lit up again and he grabbed fistfuls of whatever desserts he could. Elisabeth saw him drop one perfectly shaped *mandelkipfel* and it broke into chunks and crumbs on the floor, only to be flattened by someone passing by. She sighed. So much for that perfectly shaped cookie.

Once everyone was served, the bride was led outside, with two young children holding her train up from the snow and slush. Everyone followed behind her. The wedding parade, careful to avoid bad luck by not following the same route twice, headed for the groom's house. After-wards, everyone would go to the church for the religious ceremony, then to the town hall for the legal marriage, and finally they would celebrate with a party until the early hours of the morning.

"Elisabeth, are you coming?" Luki ran into the front room of their house and grabbed her hand. "We have to get to the *festhalle*! I think they're already dancing!" Although Luki's energy had returned from his illness, his full personality had not: he was still a little gentleman to Elisabeth.

"Yes, Luki, just hold on a moment!" she said, laughing. "If you grab my hand, I can't carry the food!"

The entire family—Mammi, Elisabeth, Anna, Luki, and Rosina—carried either a bowl or platter to take to the *festhalle* for the rest of the wedding festivities. Elisabeth's hands gripped both sides of a cake platter with her rum roll on it. Peeling it off the baking sheet had left a few rips in the cake, but buttercream icing had covered those just fine, and Elisabeth etched a few stars into it for an extra blessing. Although it was not a perfect cake, it certainly wouldn't embarrass Mammi either. Mammi carried her coffee cake, carefully balanced on top of a pot of soup; Anna carried two baskets of yeast *kipfel*, and Rosina carried some plates and cutlery.

The ceremony had been beautiful, and Elisabeth had had to wipe a few tears away herself. Susi was now married, now a woman at seventeen years of age. Next in line would come children, if God allowed, hopefully the first one before Christmas.

Luki carried everyone's dress shoes in a bag over his shoulder so they could get change into proper shoes at the *festhalle*. Mammi wouldn't dance, of course—it would be inappropriate for her to dance with another man in her husband's absence. But Elisabeth couldn't wait to see who would ask her to dance. Maybe her future husband?

"I can't wait to see all the skirts turning around on the floor!" Rosina jumped up and down in excitement and almost slipped on the packed snow.

"Careful!" Anna said with a laugh. "You won't be able to dance if your dress is soaked!"

As merry as the children were, Mammi's sadness hung like a shroud around her. Elisabeth wondered if this was what it felt like to lose someone very close to you to God. Although Mammi kept her chin up, her shoulders slumped as the family made their way through the snow to the *festhalle*. Elisabeth missed Tata, too, of course, but this time, she wondered if Mammi missed him more, especially because Konrad-Bátschi and Margarethe-Néni had already heard from him.

As they neared the hall, the music and dancing erased any concern Elisabeth had for Mammi: not because she didn't care for her, but because this was the first event she had attended since she had taken over the household, and she couldn't wait to find her friends, especially Maria.

Once inside, they carried the dinner food to the serving tables and the cakes—well-covered so no one could see them—to a table in the back corner where all the other women's fancy treats sat, waiting to be the pride or embarrassment of their creator.

NOW CAME ELISABETH'S FAVOURITE PART OF THE WHOLE DAY: when the wreath on the bride's head would be replaced by a new bonnet.

Susi's new husband, Adam, and her girlfriends and unmarried female family members, including Elisabeth and her sisters, all held hands and walked in a circle. The girls and Susi began their song:

> *Come here, come here, oh husband of mine,*
> *I want to love you until the end of time.*
> *Come here, come here, oh friends of mine,*
> *Let us have fun together, just one more time.*

The group began to close in on Susi, with Adam breaking free and standing by his new wife's side. With the next verse, the girls stepped back and then allowed a circle of married women to come forward. As Elisabeth stepped back, she couldn't help but notice Georg standing alone in a corner of the room, far away from his wife or anyone else. But Elisabeth kept singing with the group.

> *Go away, go away, oh friends of mine,*
> *Our fun must end now, it is time.*
> *Come here, come here, oh devoted wives,*
> *Take me into your arms, into your lives.*

Gretche, the eldest sister in Susi's family, lifted the white floral wreath from her sister's head. The girls continued their song:

> *Take it off, take it off, this wreath that shines,*
> *Put on, put on, this new bonnet of mine.*

Then Konrad-Bátschi and Margarethe-Néni entered the circle for the last two lines.

> *Come here, come here, oh parents of mine,*
> *I must say good-bye to you, for it is now that*
>   *time.*

Tears flowed freely down Susi's face as Margarethe-Néni pressed her hands against her daughter's cheeks and gave her one last big kiss. Elisabeth's aunt pulled a handkerchief out of her hand purse and did her best to quietly blow her nose. But her sadness overflowed so much it sounded more like a goose honk.

Elisabeth dabbed a handkerchief on her own tears. Susi was no longer one of them, no longer Schuhmacher Susi, a young girl. She was now a woman—Schubkegel Susi—and would join the world of married women and, soon, of mothers.

ELISABETH SQUEEZED OUT OF THE THRONG OF WELL-WISHERS once Susi had received her *haube* and headed straight for Georg, whose eyes were fixed on his youngest sister.

"Are you all right?"

He nodded, not taking his eyes off Susi.

"You look scared," she said.

"I don't want her to die."

Elisabeth glanced in Susi's direction and then back at Georg. Susi was dancing so merrily that it was hard to think of the day her life would end. What could Elisabeth say to help Georg feel better?

"She's happy now. She's alive and married. Shouldn't you be happy for her?"

Georg's eyes didn't move as he answered her. "But she doesn't deserve to die."

Those were hardly the words of a shameful person; they were the words of someone who cared for his family and was—for reasons Elisabeth didn't understand—very frightened. But Elisabeth couldn't figure out where his mind was: was he thinking about the war? Or about his first wife and child? Nobody deserved to die, not anyone here in Semlak, or across the world in Pennsylvania where Tata was. And Jesus certainly did not deserve to die.

Jesus...Elisabeth thought back to what she'd read in Genesis and tried again to reach her cousin.

"When Jesus died, He went up to the stars and now looks down on us. I think we do the same. We'll all die someday, Georg, and then angels will take us to Him, up to the stars where we can look down on those we leave behind."

He turned his head toward her. "Do you really believe that?"

She nodded.

"Then why did I watch my best friend die? If Jesus is looking down on us, why did He take him?"

Georg looked at her for a moment, though Elisabeth couldn't tell if he actually saw her; it was as though his eyes were looking through her instead of at her. Then he returned his gaze to his sister.

Elisabeth thought for a minute before answering. "Maybe the person who killed him had lost Jesus for that moment. Maybe he didn't hear Jesus tell him to stop shooting. Or maybe his commander didn't hear Jesus and told him to shoot, otherwise he'd be shot and would never see his family again."

In truth, Elisabeth didn't know what the answer was— Luki had seemed close to death and he had lived when other children had died. But other than Georg, Elisabeth knew of no one who became seriously ill and was healed only to turn into a very different person. As far as she could tell, war did something different to some people. Not all— Tata seemed fine—but to some.

"I'd never thought of it like that," Georg said and he seemed to mull over Elisabeth's words in his mind for another few minutes. The waltz the band was playing finished and a polka followed.

"Will you dance with me?" Georg asked, his face still showing no expression. Elisabeth smiled and accepted.

CHAPTER FIFTEEN

*I*t was Saturday, the last weekend before the end of Christmas break. Juliana was sitting on the couch in the living room, studying the drawing of the young woman who'd just been married. She couldn't believe the details her great-grandmother could draw at such a young age. The bride, tears streaming down her cheeks, looked both sad and happy.

Did she not want to get married? Had she been forced into this? Or did this drawing suggest what her great-grandmother had thought about marriage herself? Juliana knew from the times she had choreographed her own combinations in dance that her dances reflected more what she was feeling and less what she thought an audience might want to see. Did her great-grandmother draw the same way?

The stairs from the basement creaked, and judging by their heaviness and slowness, Juliana guessed it was Opa. A minute later proved she was right. She looked up at him. "Opa, can I ask you something?"

He sat down next to her, taking the book of drawings from Juliana. "Mammi's book of drawings," he said, studying the wedding scene. "Ah, this is the picture you showed your friend on the computer. I remember more about it now: the bride was one of Mammi's cousins." His crooked finger floated above the page as he inspected every corner of it. He stopped in front of the face of a man standing in a corner, singled out from all the festivities. "He's the one who had a bird in his head."

Huh? What on earth was that supposed to mean?

Upon seeing Juliana's confused face, Opa laughed. "I'm sorry—that was German. When someone's crazy, we say he has a bird in his head. This is Georg."

Juliana had read more about PTSD online, for example, that people reminded others to be mindful when cele-brating with fireworks if soldiers lived nearby because it could really disturb them. To Juliana's disgust, insensitive remarks often followed such posts. Opa's seeming lack of sensitivity similarly bothered her.

"Georg had PTSD," Juliana said.

"That fancy word of yours again."

"Post-traumatic stress disorder, Opa. It happens to

soldiers all the time. They can't cope with normal, everyday life when they come back from war."

Opa looked lost in thought for a moment and then shrugged. "I don't know—lots of men coped just fine, Mammi said. Even Ota." Then he shook his head. "No. If you can't look after your family, then you're not a man."

He looked back at the drawing and pointed to a young girl. "That's Anna-Néni when she was a girl. She was very good to me. Your Aunt Anne was named after her. Actually..." he paused, again seeming to be lost in thought. "I think Mammi said Anna-Néni couldn't wear her mittens when Georg was around, otherwise he'd get the shakes. But that's less important than the wedding. A wedding for a woman meant a new life, and that's why she got a *haube*."

Juliana thought Opa's last statement a little callous. How could a soldier suffering from PTSD be less important than a wedding? But a gut feeling told Juliana now was not the time to ask.

"You told me about the...how-ba when you met Rachel on my computer."

Opa nodded, signalling he remembered. "A bonnet. Mammi couldn't wait to have one herself. She wanted to marry and have a family." Then he looked directly at Juliana. "And when are you going to have a family?"

Juliana laughed out loud. "Me? A family? You're joking, right, Opa?"

The side door to the house opened and a draft of cold air shot through the main floor.

"You're fourteen. You should start thinking about it," Opa said.

"Opa, I've only started high school!"

"What's all the ruckus about?" Dad smiled at them as he passed by to carry his coat to the back hallway.

"Opa just asked me when I was going to get married," Juliana said.

Dad smiled. "I'm sure he's joking."

But Opa shook his head. "She's fourteen, Paul. She needs to start thinking about it, and you and Katy need to start finding her a husband."

Dad stopped for a moment, and Juliana watched his face go from happy to concerned. "Peter, where are we?"

"You don't know? In Semlak."

Judging by the look on Dad's face, Juliana knew her father was now worried.

"Peter, you haven't lived in Semlak for decades. You live in Kitchener. You left Semlak in your twenties, when your cousin arranged for you and everyone else to go to Pennsylvania, and you came here a year later."

Opa's eyes blinked a few times and then he laughed. But it was an unnatural laugh, the kind any of Juliana's friends would use to cover up something really embarrassing, like leaking through a tampon.

"I'm just joking, Paul, you know that!" He forced his

laugh some more and then got up. "Better go get some water from that well!" He slapped his knee and laughed all the way to the basement door. Standing by the doorway to the stairs, he turned around. "You know what? I'm pretty sure Mammi was fourteen when she started that book." He then faked his laugh again. "I had you there for a moment," he said, and then disappeared.

Juliana looked at Dad. "What was that all about?"

Dad's eyes grew sad. "His dementia might be further along than we thought. I think for a moment there he actually believed he was back home."

Juliana had read that people with dementia could do that and that some homes for them actually had "sets" of buildings from their younger years, like what you'd find on a Hollywood soundstage, to help keep dementia patients alert and engaged. Still others had windows painted on the backs of doors to the patients' rooms to make them think it was actually a window and not a door so they wouldn't wander away.

But she'd only really met her grandfather when they moved here. Before that, their only contact had been the odd stilted phone call and kitschy greeting cards. He really cared about her, and even if she didn't agree with everything he said, he had a lifetime of information about her family's past. How would she learn it all before his dementia took over completely?

"What's that?" Dad pointed to the book, sat down, and picked it up.

"It's what I found in the basement," Juliana said. She hadn't shown it to Dad or Mom yet, and apparently Opa hadn't said anything either. "They're from Opa's mom. So far as I know, she drew these pictures based on what was happening in her life. Don't touch the drawings, though. Opa says they'll smudge."

Dad gently flipped through the pages and stopped at one about halfway through: a man was lying down on some kind of simple, open coffin, his hands folded over his chest, his eyes closed. Nine people stood behind the coffin, their hands folded in prayer, looking solemnly in the artist's direction.

"Is he dead?" Dad asked.

Juliana studied the drawing more closely. "I think so. Man, that's creepy, eh?"

"You know, I think your mom mentioned once that they used to take pictures like this so they could send copies to any family abroad." He shuddered, and so did Juliana. Then they both laughed.

"But wait, Dad, look," and Juliana pointed to a few watermarks on the page. "Are those tears?"

Dad held the book a little closer to his face. "I think you're right. Wow." And both sat in silence for a moment. Juliana could even sense that rope that connected them returning.

Dad continued. "I love your mom, but her ancestors... they could sometimes be really strange. Let's turn to another page. What's the drawing you were looking at?"

Juliana flipped back to the picture of the wedding and explained to Dad what she knew.

"And they apparently do this ritual where she says good-bye to her friends, because she'll no longer hang out with them because she's now a wife. Isn't that horrible?"

Dad thought for a moment. "I'm sure she wouldn't stop hanging out with them, but I can understand if she spent more time with other wives than her unmarried friends. I think it depends on how you look at it. Maybe it's backwards by our standards, but it's not much different from the party Miss Kasia threw you in Calgary. You weren't getting married, but you were starting a new life and saying goodbye to your friends. Farewell parties are one ritual we have and it's kind of the same. Your high school graduation will be like that, too."

Juliana had to admit that Dad had a point. But she wasn't going to let him win the entire argument.

"But check out this guy." She pointed to Georg and told Dad what Opa had said about him. "Opa wouldn't change his mind once I explained things to him: he still believes Georg didn't care for his family. I don't get it."

The expression on Dad's face changed abruptly, and Juliana couldn't tell why. He set the book down on the coffee table, walked over to the bay window, and looked out to the street. The only sound Juliana could hear was him breathing.

"Dad?"

He shook his head. "People don't get what war can do to a man—or a woman, of course, but in your Opa's time, only men would've been accused of being lazy, shameful, all that crap. He doesn't know what it's like to grow up with a father who..." He lifted a hand to his face, and through his reflection in the window, Juliana could see him wipe away tears. Had Dad's father suffered from PTSD? She had no idea Dad's childhood had been so difficult. Juliana regretted all the things she'd accused Dad of recently. She needed to say something, but what?

"I'm...um...well..." Nothing intelligent came out of her mouth.

He sniffled and dried his eyes. "I know, you don't like mushy stuff," he said, as though he'd read her thoughts. He turned around to face her, and his eyes were red. "But you're my daughter. I don't know if you'll have a family someday or not, but I hope to God you'll never have to lose anyone to war." Dad pulled a Kleenex from his pocket and wiped his nose. "I'd better pack. After I drop you off at school on Monday, I head out of town on my first trip."

Juliana's heart sank. She and Dad argued a lot, but something good had clicked during the holidays. Why did he have to leave now? Maybe the reason they didn't argue as much was because he was actually around. Would it be more peaceful at home if he didn't have to leave so often?

"How long is this one?"

"I'm driving down to Florida. I'll be gone about five days." He patted Juliana on the shoulder. "Don't worry, I won't hug you. But you do need to know that both your mom and I love you, and that we're doing all of this for you." He didn't wait for a response, which relieved Juliana because she had none, and he headed to his bedroom. But before he disappeared down the hallway, he said, "And please don't think about marriage. Heck, don't even think about dating!"

CHAPTER SIXTEEN

*W*ith the wedding several days before and the first week of February now coming to an end, Elisabeth hoped she could finally rest—at least she wouldn't have to add all those wedding responsibilities to her already busy days. But alas, now she lay in bed with a fever and a cough.

And so did Anna.

And so did Rosina.

The front room was never quiet—someone was always coughing—which made it hard for anyone to sleep. Mammi ran faster than a galloping horse between the workshop and her children, getting them tea, broths—anything they needed—and finishing a customer's pair of shoes.

Surprisingly, eight-year-old Luki took on the role of

caregiver in the family whenever Mammi wasn't in the house. Although he was too young to boil water, he set out dried teas, sliced very wide, uneven pieces of bread for the girls, and otherwise tended to them.

The house door opened with a bang and Mammi came running in.

"We're fine, Mammi," Elisabeth said, assuming Mammi was assuming the worst. She coughed. "Luki's looking after us."

But Mammi had something in her hand: a letter.

"Your father has finally written us," she said, her eyes moist with happiness. "He writes that he has found work in a cigar factory. It stinks and he has to ask the people he's staying with to not smoke while he's home—the smell makes him sick—but it is a good job." Mammi smiled and then looked at her four children. "Your father is a good man." She continued reporting on the letter. "He is tired after very long days working in the factory but sometimes he still makes shoes in the evenings. And so long as God gives him strength, he'll keep working. He wants to earn money for land and a shingle roof for us, and also to help Elisabeth marry well. That will save money for the two of you." She nodded at Anna and Rosina, and then sniffled and wiped her nose with a handkerchief. "He hopes to be back before it's time for Elisabeth to marry."

Rosina coughed, followed by Anna, and then Elisabeth. They looked up at Mammi, who said nothing more.

"Is that it?" Elisabeth asked. "Is that all he wrote?"

Mammi nodded. "It is very little, but I have his address now so we may write him. Jesus has watched over our family and protected Tata. We must be thankful and continue to work hard."

Luki jumped up and down. "Daddy's alive!"

Mammi nodded, a small smile on her face. "Luki, it's time you began to learn your father's trade. Get your coat and follow me."

"No," he said, his old personality having finally returned.

Mammi's eyes flared. "What did you say?" Mammi's personality had also been restored.

"I said, no! Tata will teach me!"

Mammi would not have it. She grabbed her son by the arm, and his little body was no match for hers. "Your Tata is not here," she said through gritted teeth. "Now let's get your boots and coat." She pinched Luki by the ear and pulled him into the back room.

DAY FIVE AND ELISABETH'S FEVER HAD FINALLY BROKEN AND her strength was beginning to return. She gave Jesus a prayer of thanks for her fast recovery. Mammi had taken over these past few days, cooking and shoemaking, but said she would leave the cleaning and laundry to Elisabeth once she got well. Elisabeth noticed that Mammi didn't look well herself during those days, but as always, Mammi made nothing of it and kept pushing on. Elisabeth could only hope she wouldn't have to care for her mother, not yet, anyway. Mammi was still too young for that.

Elisabeth sat propped up in her bed, her knees bent and her drawing book in her lap. She was shading in Susi's face. So far as she knew, her cousin had been happy to be married, but Elisabeth couldn't help but wonder if she was also sad to leave her parents' home and her life as she knew it. No young woman knew what moving in with her new husband would be like, and Elisabeth had heard rumours that it wasn't always nice. But to be seen as a woman and respected as one must be exhilarating, too.

She held the book away from her and studied her work. "I do draw well," she whispered to herself. "It's too bad I can't earn money from this."

She set the book back on her lap and turned to the previous drawing of Georg's hands trying to pull off Anna's mittens.

"I don't know how to draw fear into his hands," she said. "Not yet, anyway." She studied her drawing some more. "But these hands are too clean, like those of a city shopkeeper, perhaps." And she shaded in some black stains to better show his blacksmithing work.

She thought about Georg and looked up at Jesus on the crucifix. "How come he gets to earn money by creating and

I don't?" Elisabeth knew that almost all Lutheran Semlakers were farmers. It wasn't so much that she was questioning that but more wondering why Georg could be paid to hammer out physical pictures—that's what black-smithing looked like to her—but she could not earn money drawing pictures on paper. Then she shook her head.

"Elisabeth, what a silly question. How does drawing help people survive? I'm only doing this because I enjoy it and so that Tata can see what happened while he is away."

She flipped back to the wedding and began to draw Georg in the corner, watching the crowd but fearing it at the same time. As she drew his face, she couldn't imagine how Eva could be happy in a marriage to Georg. Secure, most likely, but happy?

But then, marriages were blessed by Jesus, and if Jesus was indeed looking down upon everyone, He obviously allowed unhappy marriages to happen. And Jesus was never wrong, according to Pastor Fröhlich's teachings. Elisabeth had to conclude that happiness in a marriage really didn't matter.

A knock at the house door got Elisabeth out of bed. Anna and Rosina were sleeping—they were healing well but not as quickly as Elisabeth—so she closed the door to the front room behind her and then opened the house door in the kitchen.

"Maria!"

Her friend entered, again holding a pot of soup. "I came

down with a fever a few days before you did. But I'd heard from Meier Josef that you weren't healthy yet, so here I am again!"

"Your family has been so good to us," Elisabeth said. "Once this sickness is over, we'll have you over to say thank you." Elisabeth coughed.

"Don't worry about any of that," Maria said. "You sit down and I'll serve you."

Elisabeth didn't object.

"But I also have some news to share with you."

"Oh?"

"Herr Blum is sick now: he had to send all the children home today."

Herr Blum was the teacher for the one-room school that held grades three to six. This meant he would be off for close to a week, maybe more.

And that meant Elisabeth would have to look after all her siblings by herself until Herr Blum returned to school. Suddenly, looking after one sick child seemed as easy as cooking goulash.

CHAPTER SEVENTEEN

*J*uliana wiped the sweat off her brow while she sat on the thick carpet, stretching to cool down. School—and her new weekly schedule—started tomorrow. Although she finally knew most of the tap routine, she'd start learning the jazz number this week, on top of having to study for exams. Jasmine had also given her a few good tips on how to improve her balance on her pirouettes, and they were working! She pushed the tap board under the couch and headed upstairs. She stopped when she heard Dad say, "We just started to connect."

"And now you're leaving again," Mom said.

There was a pause followed by one of Dad's sighs. "The distance really is ruining my relationship with her," he said, "and with your work hours...I don't know. I'm worried she'll be the one left looking after your father."

Another pause.

"Maybe we didn't think this through enough," Mom said. "It seemed like a good idea at the time."

Another sigh. But inside Juliana, panic broke out. She was just getting used to being here! She finally had everything organized and had already learned one competition routine out of five! Go back to Calgary? Juliana had to admit she didn't know what she'd prefer right now.

"But we're here," Dad said. "We can't go back. Your family is depending on us to care for your dad, and your sister is still far too busy to step in." Juliana relaxed. "And if there's one thing you've always said it's that you'd always come back here someday, just like your Oma eventually returned to Semlak with your father. We're here. Let's go ahead with everything we have planned, but maybe it's time I finally start looking into another kind of job; something that will let me stay home more often, maybe let me have a regular schedule. Our expenses are a lot lower now, so we can afford my starting fresh."

"But honey, you can't start with a new employer and then just quit."

"I know, and I won't. But starting a new career takes time, and maybe there's, I don't know, courses or something I can take while I'm on the road."

"But school was never your strong point."

Another sigh and then a light laugh. "Maybe Juliana can help me with that."

A pause. And then a noisy kiss. Juliana recoiled in horror. Parents weren't supposed to kiss: that was just gross.

But the conversation was over. Juliana showered in the basement so her parents wouldn't know she'd been eavesdropping and then made herself a snack in the kitchen. Back in her room, she began packing her backpack for school. She started at her new school, Eby Heights, tomorrow. If it hadn't been for her dance practice sessions, she knew she'd be jumping up and down like popcorn right now, full of nervous energy. Instead, her exhaustion made her feel more like melted butter.

A familiar ring sounded on her phone and laptop. Juliana stuck in her earbuds and answered the call.

"Rachel!"

"Jules! I haven't heard from you in a few days! Thought I'd check in! See if you've decided what to do with your life!"

Juliana laughed: Rachel could always be counted on to get her smiling. She told her about her conversations with Dad and Opa but said nothing about the new studio or Jasmine. She had spent hours practicing, more than she would have at home in fact, just to begin to catch up. She saw the difference already, and she'd be lying to herself if she didn't admit that it did feel good. Maybe this studio would be better than Miss Kasia's back in Calgary.

"No way..." Rachel said, in response to Juliana's story about Dad's parents. "Your dad's gone through a lot, sure, but he's pretty normal as far as dads go."

"I know. He's almost boring." She giggled kindly. "But you know what? We actually connected. I know I'm not supposed to say this—he's my dad and I'm his teenager— but I kind of liked it. I had no idea about his family, and I think it really hurts him to talk about them."

"Wow. Who knew?"

"And then there's school," Juliana said, wanting to change the topic before Rachel asked about her studio. "It's a really old building with a huge addition on the back and a ton of portables. The winter is going to be brutal in those. This wet cold gets into your bones."

Rachel mimicked a shiver. "That sounds awful! And what about your exams? How's that going to work?"

Juliana rested her elbows on her desk and explained what she knew.

There was a knock on the door and Dad entered. He waved at Rachel and Juliana pulled the earbud jack out of her laptop so her father and best friend could talk.

"Hi, Rachel," he said. "How are you?"

"I'm fine, thank you."

"Good to hear. Listen, I need to talk to Juliana about a few things. Can she call you back?"

"Sure!"

Both best friends gave each other a look that confirmed

Rachel would be waiting by her computer, and then they hung up.

"Sorry to interrupt you, but Mom and I will be heading out to the mall shortly for some last-minute shopping before it closes. I wanted to see if you needed anything for tomorrow."

Juliana pulled out her agenda and opened it to a page of notes. "I haven't checked everything off yet, but..." She ran through her packing list, rummaged around in her backpack a bit, and then closed the book. "I think I've got everything."

"Paul! Are you coming?" Mom called from the kitchen.

"Be right there!" he replied. "Listen. Neither your mom nor I expected this move to be easy, but that doesn't mean it has to be hard. You have my cell phone, and I'll have my earpiece in while I'm on the road. You call me if you need me, okay? Any time. Day or night."

Juliana nodded, signalling she'd heard him.

"And we'll be getting take-out for supper. Sushi?"

Juliana's nod turned into an enthusiastic yes.

"I'll see you later," Dad said and left.

Juliana immediately called Rachel back.

"And?"

"Man, I wish he weren't leaving again so soon."

"Jules, if there's one thing I learned about my parents' divorce, it's that sometimes it's easiest to just accept things as they are."

Juliana nodded in resignation. When Rachel was right, she was right.

The two kept talking and talking...about school, parents, their favourite cheesy Christmas TV movies, and about missing each other. Juliana didn't talk about her new studio, and to her surprise, Rachel didn't ask about it. Was she also scared that something would split them apart?

Eventually Rachel asked that very question a good hour into the conversation. "Nothing will come between us, right, Jules?"

Just then, Juliana's phone vibrated and a notification came up on her laptop screen.

It's Jasmine. Practice at my place this aft? Turns out we live close to each other.

"What was that?" Rachel asked.

"Uh, nothing." But Jasmine's request hung in Juliana's mind. It would be nice to have a new friend here in town, and especially so soon after moving here.

"Juliana?"

"Um, I should get going. I've got lots to prep for school tomorrow."

Rachel looked crestfallen. "Oh. Okay."

"You're my best friend, Rachel. I promise to call you tomorrow night, okay? After supper my time, after school your time?"

Rachel nodded. They said their goodbyes and hung up.

Juliana replied to Jasmine.

Sorry—on the phone. Sounds good! What time?

1 hour?

Sure!

Jasmine sent through her address.

Juliana then reached for her book of goals and opened it.

✓ *Make 5 new friends in January and keep them*

Would Jasmine be the first one? Juliana hoped so.

SETTING THE RECORD
STRAIGHT

Between Worlds is historical fiction: the story is the backbone of a historical fiction book, but it's based on actual historical events. To learn more about some of the historical aspects of the story, read below. (You'll also find more information in the other books in the series.)

NAMES

Naming conventions in Semlak and other German towns in Eastern Europe were actually quite complex because so many people shared the same names. For example, in the roughly 2,700 families that made up the Lutheran congregation from 1819-2000, 1,000 of them shared just 10 last names. During that same time period, 411 boys were named Adam, 334 Heinrich, 421 Martin, and 534 Andreas. On the girls' side, 783 were named Elisabeth, 530 Susanna, and 196 Anna. (As a side note, "Lukas" was not a name listed in the Lutheran church books. I wanted a Biblical name and then made up the short form "Luki.")

To reduce confusion, these cultures developed patterns to name everyone more clearly. Some examples of naming patterns given in the book *Semlak*, edited by Georg Schmidt, include the following:

- *Arva-Schuster:* his last name was Arva and he was a shoemaker. ("Shoemaker" is both "Schuhmacher" and "Schuster" in German, depending on the region.)
- *Stielche-Schuster:* this is something that wouldn't happen today. He was a shoemaker but required a small chair to get around (i.e., like a walker). "Stielche" is a word in the Semlak Lutheran dialect that means "little chair."
- *Paprika-Rosza:* a gardener who planted peppers.
- *Eck-Néni:* literally, Aunt Corner. The woman's name was actually Elisabeth Tichy, but her house was on a corner.

"Néni" and "Bátschi," though Hungarian for "aunt" and "uncle," were also used as forms of address for anyone within one's familiar circles.

In chapter 10, Elisabeth is thinking about naming

conventions in her family: Anna was born a twin, but Rosina died, and so Mammi gave the name to the next live birth that was a girl. I have an ancestor named Elisabeth, and she gave birth to four daughters, each named Elisabeth. Sadly, none survived, which is why I chose Elisabeth for the name of the historical protagonist.

SICKNESS

Sickness was dealt with differently in Elisabeth's culture than today in North America. For example, even if someone was already burning up, they may have still been covered up so they could sweat it out. As you likely know, this is not the way to go these days: if you have a fever, you might actually take medicine to bring it down, and if your fever is high, you may even go to the hospital. If your fever can be managed at home, your parents or doctor may also suggest that you wear only thin layers, like a summer PJ, so you don't heat up anymore: a high fever can lead to complications, and in Elisabeth's day, this happened often and could result in death.

TRANSLATION

It's easy to think that translation is about just finding the single word you're looking for. For example, when you learn French, you learn that "Comment ça va?" means

"How are you?" in English. But if you look at it closely, it actually says, "How it goes?" German is similar: "Wie geht's?" literally means "How goes it?" The intent of the question is to ask after your well-being, and so what you learn in foreign language classes is a phrase that functions in the same way in English, even if the words are actually a little different.

The song the wedding guests sing in chapter 14 is this, taken from the book *Semlak*:

> *Trete bei, trete bei mein Ehemann,*
> *Dich will ich lieben mein Leben lang.*
> *Tretet bei, tretet bei ihr Kameraden mein,*
> *Mit euch will ich noch einmal lustig sein.*
>
> *Tretet ab, tretet ab ihr Kameraden mein,*
> *Mit euch kann ich nicht mehr lustig sein.*
> *Tretet bei, tretet bei ihr Weiberlein,*
> *Schließt mich in eure Gesellschaft ein.*
>
> *Nehmet ab, nehmet ab das Kränzelein,*
> *Setzet auf, setzet auf das Häubelein.*
> *Tretet bei, tretet bei, liebe Eltern mein,*
> *Von Euch muss ich jetzt geschieden sein.*

If I were to translate that word for word, it could look something like this:

Step next to me, step next to me, my husband,
I want to love you my whole life long.
Step next to me, step next to me, my comrades,
I want to be funny with you one more time.

Step away, step away, you comrades of mine,
I can no longer be funny with you.
Step next to me, step next to me, you little wives,
And lock me into your society.

Take away, take away this little wreath,
Put on, put on the little bonnet.
Step next to me, step next to me, my dear
    parents,
I must now be split from you.

It doesn't work well, does it? It's because I didn't use any context to do the translation; I simply picked English translations that were often taught in textbooks. If you know German, you may even suggest other translations instead of what I've written here. For example, the last line, "Von Euch muss ich jetzt geschieden sein," could mean, "From you [plural] I must now be divorced," because "geschieden" can be used as an adjective to say someone is divorced. However, I think you'd agree with me that, within the context of this ritual, "divorced" is the wrong word.

I settled for an interpretation of this song in such a way

that you would read it as a song and understand a ritual that marked a single woman's transition into marriage.

To see how much translation can change the meaning, feel free to run part of the poem or all of it through an online translator and see what happens. And if you'd like to share your findings, you can post them on my Facebook page (www.facebook.com/loriwolfheffner) or ping me on your tweet (@ltmStraus).

(And for some extra fun, visit Translator Fails on Youtube. She runs well-known songs several times through Google Translate and then sings them.)

STAY IN TOUCH!

If you enjoyed the book, sign up for my monthly newsletter! I write it myself, so it's my words to you. You'll get the following:

- Sneak peeks at upcoming books
- Updates about online and in-person appearances
- Book and writing recommendations
- Recipes I love
- Contests
- And more!

Visit BetweenWorldsYA.com to sign up!

Prefer social media? All my links are listed under my bio, at the end of the book.

COLLECT ALL THE BOOKS IN THE SERIES

Don't miss out on a single step in Juliana's and Elisabeth's journeys. You can order the books below from your favourite book store or online retailer.

AVAILABLE IN REGULAR PRINT, LARGE PRINT, AND EBOOK

1. The Move
2. The Distance
3. The First Step
4. What Friends Do
5. Hide and Seek
6. Missing Home
7. What Will Come
8. A Father's Journey
9. The last book! Coming in 2023.

ACKNOWLEDGEMENTS

First off, thank you to all who purchased the first book in this series, *Between Worlds 1: The Move*. Hearing your feedback helped shape this book.

Next, I'd like to thank the following people for their help and support:

Mom & Dad; Kristin; Deardra King-Leslie; Heather Wright, my consulting editor and writing coach; Susan Fish, my editor; Michelle Fairbanks of Fresh Design, my graphics designer; the Heimatortsgemeinschaft Semlak; Kyle Bergum; Ali MacGee; Donauschwaben Villages Helping Hands; Nick Tullius; Tom Harding and Helena Calogeridis from the Dana Porter Library at the University of Waterloo; and finally, my husband, Corey; and two sons, Khristopher and Jonnathan.

Contrary to popular belief and mythology, books don't get written alone, and without the help of the above people and organizations, this book may have remained little more than an idea in the back of my mind. Thank you for being a part of my journey.

ABOUT LORI

Photo by Erin Watt Photography

Lori Wolf-Heffner is a former competitive dancer, dance teacher, and theatre manager. She was a member of the first Canadian National Tap Team, back in 1996, under the leadership of Bonnie Dyer, with choreographer Mathew Clark. She's written for *Dance Canada Quarterly*, *just dance!* magazine, and *The Dance Current* (all under Lori Straus).

Fluent in German, Lori lived in Germany for three years, never once realizing just how close she was to some of the villages her ancestors left to migrate to Eastern Europe in the 1700s.

Lori lives in Waterloo, Ontario, Canada, with her

husband and two sons. She is a member of The Writers' Union of Canada and the Alliance of Independent Authors.

facebook.com/loriwolfheffner

twitter.com/LoriWolfHeffner

instagram.com/loriwolfheffner

goodreads.com/lori_wolf-heffner

bookbub.com/author/lori-wolf-heffner

pinterest.com/loriwolfheffner

amazon.com/author/loriwolfheffner